HELD

ISABELLE TAYLOR

Publisher's Note: This is a work of fiction. Names, characters, places, and incidents are a product of the author's imagination. Locales and public names are sometimes used for atmospheric purposes. Any resemblance to actual people, living or dead, or to businesses, companies, events, institutions, or locales is completely coincidental.

KDP Paperback ISBN: 979-8-285091-17-2

IngramSpark Paperback ISBN: 978-1-067061-74-6

IngramSpark Hardcover ISBN: 978-1-067061-75-3

CONTENT WARNINGS

Loss of virginity (it's the monster this time), Fuck-Or-Die, anal penetration, limb amputation, inhuman penis (it has ridges), animal death, public sex, ritualistic sex, graphic burns, animal death.

ONE

Briar was running out of time.

She looked around the dark tavern with a confident smirk, something she didn't feel in the slightest. Appearances were important: she could hardly show the desperation that started kicking in after sunset, another constant reminder of how close she was to dying right here in this grimy tavern.

Unless she found a lover. If she could find someone to sleep with before midnight, she would be granted another day. Thanks to that gods-damned wizard who couldn't take no for an answer and was very promptly killed for it, only to choke out his curse with his dying words.

That was months ago. There wasn't a day that went by when Briar didn't wish she had killed him faster. Sex was fun, to be sure. But she was getting deeply tired of finding someone new every night.

Briar checked that her pack was still next to her feet

and gave the tavern another annoyed glance. Still, no one was interested—she'd already done the rounds, only to find a eunuch, an irritatingly loyal husband, and a man who assumed she wanted to pickpocket him. Which, to be fair, wasn't entirely off the mark. She had been planning on stealing his coin purse afterward.

After months of traveling from town to town, she was almost at the point of no return. Right next to the town waited an endless stretch of forest that Briar had to travel through to meet Marigold, Briar's only hope of lifting her curse. If she had come to the last small town, then she had to find some poor fool who was horny or stupid enough to follow her for weeks through a perilous forest in exchange for fucking her every night.

The tavern door creaked open. Briar looked up, her smile turning genuine as she noticed a new man. A tall, sturdy man with no companion. The perfect mark.

She waited for him to take a seat at the other end of the bar. Then she picked up her pack and walked over, making sure to make her hips swing as she went.

"Hello," she said coolly as she dropped her back and slid into the stool next to him, right in front of the crackling fire. "What brings a man like you to a place like this?"

He turned to her. He was wearing a hood that covered most of his face, which was probably for the best. She'd slept with some truly ugly men since this curse took hold. Sometimes it was better not to see too much.

The man said nothing. He held up a hand, and the

bartender slid a glass of moonshine in front of him without asking.

A local, Briar decided. And a working man, if his scarred hands and the weapons hanging off his belt were anything to go by. There was something familiar about him, but she couldn't put her finger on what.

She leaned forward coyly as she toyed with her necklace: a white gemstone amulet that Marigold had given her during simpler times. Briar was never a sentimental woman, but she had allowed herself this one keepsake. She usually kept it tucked away—better to have nothing people could recognize you by.

"I only ask because I'm looking for a man like you," she said, dragging her fingers seductively down the necklace chain. "My bed is awfully cold tonight."

She usually warmed men up more beforehand. But the night was getting awfully long, and she could feel the curse creeping up her skin. It felt like fire, crackling and throwing sparks just like the fireplace they were sitting next to. The closer she got to midnight, the more painful it became.

Right now, it was a low simmer. Soon, it would roar into a wildfire.

She waited for the man to huff in amusement or get suspicious. Maybe ask if she was charging by the hour. Most did, if she came on this strongly.

But the man just took a sip of his drink and looked at her again.

"Salaros's family will be glad to see the curse is still in full effect," he said in a familiar voice that made her teeth clench and her blood freeze. "And after all that talk you had about undoing it."

Briar sat back, forcing her grin to stay in place. She should have known—he smelled faintly of lipseed, a crucial ingredient in the hair oil he used so copiously.

"Renault," she said chirpily, subtly scanning the tavern for exits. She had a knife in her pack, but that was it. Escape was her best bet. Escape, recoup, and find someone to accompany her through weeks' worth of forest so she wouldn't die on her first night un-fucked.

"What a nice surprise," she continued, pulling her pack subtly closer with her feet. "Is it just you this time, or did you bring your band of merry bounty hunters?"

Renault laughed, pulling his hood away to reveal the boyish smile and wavy, lipseed-smelling hair that had enchanted her for about an hour at a party when she was six and twenty. The night had ended in a blur of blood and stolen gold, both of them laughing. She had been proud that her laugh had been believable, even when she cleaned the blood off her hands afterward.

It had been almost ten years since then. Renault's path had diverted from hers, but they both revolved around money. Unfortunately for her, he had found tons of it by chasing down anyone with a bounty on their heads.

Like her. The warlock, Salaros, apparently had a very wealthy family across the sea. All the more reason to wish she'd never met the bastard. Not only did he ruin her life with this curse, but he also made her run from people like Renault and his band of hunters.

"I do enjoy our chats," Renault said, his straight teeth shining in the dim tavern firelight. "Usually when I meet a mark, it's all pleas or threats. Not you."

"Not me," Briar agreed. She eyed the fireplace next to them, keeping her smile as flirtatious as ever, even as the dread set in. This was not the time to let her guard down. She'd made it out of worse situations. Especially if he really was alone, like she suspected. Renault never liked to share his reward. She'd found that out the hard way.

She leaned in, watching him stiffen in preparation. It lasted barely a moment—he knew the importance of looking calm and confident as well as she did. But he also knew what she was capable of.

"Look," she said, trailing her finger down her necklace chain. "Salaros deserved it. You would have done the same thing, Renault."

"Probably," Renault acknowledged. He ran a finger around the ring of his glass and tapped thoughtfully. "But that's not what this is about. It's not personal. It's just about the money. You understand. If our roles were reversed..."

He paused, giving her a knowing look. "You would have done the same thing I'm about to do."

Briar leaned in closer, letting her long blonde hair brush his arm. "And what are you about to do, Ren?"

His gaze dropped to her mouth. It was gratifying, in a sad sort of way. She still had an effect on him, even after all this time. It was lucky she was so good at this. She wouldn't be alive if she weren't.

"First," Renault started.

Briar grabbed his glass and lobbed it into the fireplace.

The glass exploded, showering Renault in fiery shards.

Renault yelped, jerking out of his stool.

Briar grabbed her pack and ran. She ignored the shocked looks of the tavern-goers, Renault cursing behind her as he righted himself and shook flames off his cloak.

She burst out of the tavern. The town was dark, but she always knew how to get out of any place she was staying. She ran down the cobbled street toward the inn she'd been staying—

And staggered to a stop.

A group of men and women stepped out from around the corner. They were all wearing the same thick cloaks as Renault, carrying an array of weapons that marked them as fellow bounty hunters.

Briar swore and turned onto a side street. It was a small town, so she could already see the forest in the distance. But she could also hear the men behind her, calling to each other as they chased her.

"Get ahead of her," Renault yelled. "Told you she's a slippery one!"

Briar gritted her teeth and ran faster. She hoped she'd injured Renault with that stunt in the tavern. She thought she felt a sting of glass in her arm, but she didn't bother checking as she sped toward the dark forest.

. . .

They were still in pursuit when she hit the tree line.

She could hear them. She still hadn't glanced back yet. Looking back would get you killed. One of the many gems of wisdom she'd learned during her childhood on the streets.

They were getting closer. There was no way she'd shake them now. Even the ones who were yelling reminders about the warnings the locals had given them.

The locals had warned Briar, too.

Danger lives in those woods, they had said. *There's a cave, not far from the east entrance. There is only death and horror. Never go there.*

Briar was nothing if not a rebel. If she couldn't take on those men, maybe good ol' *death and horror* could do it for her.

And if she died in the process... well, she was going to die at midnight anyway if she didn't find a man to fuck her. Might as well take out some bounty hunters before the curse took hold.

She panted hard, eyes straining in the dim moonlight. She could almost make out the entrance of the cave. Hopefully there was a pissed off bear waiting to be woken up. Or a kobald, which was more likely considering how terrified the locals were. Maybe a demon or spirit bleeding through the voids. Forests were notorious for having thin veils between the human realm and the voids, each void nastier than the last.

She sprinted into the cave and stopped, letting out a scream that was guaranteed to wake any bear, demon, or kobald that was trying to sleep. She kept her smile in place, bright and vicious. But she also reached for the knife in her pack, just in case.

A huge shape lumbered into view. Briar's smile dropped instantly.

"Oh shit," she whispered.

It wasn't a bear. Or a kobald. She'd even take a spirit, or a demon who spat fire, *anything* but the thing in front of her.

The Skullstalker blinked. It was twice as tall as a human man, with huge horns and jagged claws and a long, whippy tail. Its skull mark was ghostly white, cutting off just above its fang-filled mouth. Shadows crept out behind the bone in ways Briar had only seen in nightmares. It had strange black markings between its chin and chest and massive spiky wings folded behind its back, both traits she hadn't heard of in Skullstalkers before. Its eyes were huge and fiery, surrounded by darkness that matched the long, black loincloth tied around its waist. The loincloth was one of the only markers that it wasn't a mindless beast. No, Skullstalkers were infinitely worse: they were intelligent, horrible beings who would devour you as soon as they looked at you.

Briar stood frozen, uncharacteristically shocked still. Usually, she had enough preservation to run. But she couldn't help it: she never thought she'd see a Skullstalker in the flesh. With its bright fangs, sharp claws, and towering stature, it was like looking death in the face.

The Skullstalker cocked its head. It looked oddly... meek. Like it was curious about her rather than ravenous.

Then something impossible happened.

"Hello," said the Skullstalker, surprised.

Briar squeaked. Sense flooded back into her, and she prepared to run.

"Wait," said the Skullstalker. Its voice was deep and gruff and oddly... polite.

An arrow slammed into the Skullstalker's shoulder. It rocked back slightly, head jerking up to see the bounty hunters closing in on the cave.

Any meekness it had displayed drained out in an instant. Its inky eyes flickered blood-red. It hunched over, its huge body shaking. Its wings snapped out, scraping the cave walls.

Briar ran out like death was on her heels. Which, in her defense, it was. If the Skullstalker didn't get her, the curse would. She could feel the fire climbing her bones, working toward her heart.

The Skullstalker emerged into the woods with a mighty bellow. Horrified yells echoed it, and arrow after arrow sailed toward the monster. It reared out with its wing and knocked a bounty hunter into a tree, snapping the trunk in half.

"Help, damn you," Renault screamed at Briar. "Or we'll all be killed!"

Briar ignored him. She'd achieved her task; they were too distracted to care about her. Now she just needed to find someplace safe.

She ran as fast as she could, fingers locked around her pack straps, lungs burning in a way that had nothing to do with the curse slowly taking hold. She just had to hope the Skullstalker was too busy with the bounty hunters to bother chasing her down. If she could just outrun it before it noticed her again—

A loud flap of wings made her stifle a frightened yell. The bounty hunters were still clamoring, Renault was shouting at them to get out, but they were getting further away.

The wings, however, were getting ever closer.

Don't look back, Briar told herself as she ran. *Don't look—*

She looked back. Barely a second, but enough to see the horrifying blur coming at her.

Clawed hands closed around her shoulders. Briar didn't even have time to reach for her weapons before it was slamming her into the dirt, her pack wedged painfully under her back. All the air whooshed painfully out of her lungs.

The Skullstalker reared up and roared, fangs glinting. Its eyes were still blood-red, its wings flared out to block the moon from view.

So, this is how I die, Briar thought, dazed. *It's even more dramatic than I expected.*

The Skullstalker lunged.

Briar squeezed her eyes shut.

A bright glow lit up the darkness. For a confused moment, Briar thought the monster had folded in its wings, letting the moonlight through.

No fangs closed around her face. No claws tore into her throat.

Briar pried her eyes open.

The Skullstalker's eyes were black again, reflecting the white light between them.

Briar looked down. That bright light wasn't the moon. It was her amulet, glowing milky white in the dark.

The Skullstalker shuddered. Briar tensed, waiting. At least she wouldn't go the way of the curse, burning from the inside out.

"Hurt me," the Skullstalker growled.

Briar paused. This monster seemed intent on saying impossible things tonight. Was this a trick? A monster playing with its food?

"What?" Briar asked weakly.

"Hurt me," it repeated. It struggled up, kneeling over her, twitching all the while. "I cannot—control—my blood. Hurt me and r—run."

Briar gaped. Then she grabbed for her pack, the knife still stuck inside. But before she could unsheath it, the Skullstalker shuddered again, a whole-body spasm.

Its thick arm banged into her skull. Briar's head bounced against the dirt, her vision tunneling as she sank into unconsciousness.

Two

When Wick awoke from his blood frenzy, the hunters had fled.

This was good. Wick did not want to surrender to yet another frenzy. Especially after the mysterious way his last one ended.

He stared at the human in disbelief. He'd carried her to his nest in the depths of his cave, not knowing where else to put her. Her amulet was no longer glowing, and yet the frenzy didn't return. He only wished he hadn't knocked her out when he was shaking it off.

Wick sat down in the nest next to her, considering. His shoulder twinged where the hunter had shot him, but with the arrow taken out, it was barely a scratch. He was more concerned with the unconscious human, whose pale brow kept furrowing in sleep. He knew very little about humans. He could not figure out why she wouldn't wake or why she went to sleep when he struck her accidentally in the head.

Maybe they go to sleep if you hit their head in a specific spot, he thought, stroking his horns thoughtfully. He had fuzzy memories of striking mortals during blood frenzies, but that generally ended with their skulls open on the ground. *Her* skull was perfectly intact. He had checked. Her head was incredibly light in his grip. He could have crushed her entire body with little effort.

The mortal made a soft noise. Wick immediately banished any thought of crushing her and sat back.

The mortal's brow scrunched yet again. Her eyes fluttered open, and Wick marveled. They were as blue as the bottom of a lake.

Those blue eyes filled with horror. She sat up, fumbling a knife from her pack before scrambling back until she hit the edge of the nest.

Wick raised a clawed hand in greeting. Mortals did that sometimes; he had seen them do it from a distance.

"Hello," he said, as politely as he could manage.

The mortal said nothing. She glanced around at the nest, her hand remarkably steady around her knife. Her other hand curled against the nest, catching on the feathers and furs he had spent so much time collecting. She stank of fear, and not for the first time, Wick wished he didn't have such a sensitive nose.

"You were asleep," Wick explained. "The other humans fled. I only killed one of them."

The human laughed. Strangely, she smelled much more panicked than she looked.

"I wish you'd killed more," she said hoarsely.

"I would have. But your amulet broke my blood frenzy." Wick gestured at the amulet hanging from a chain around her neck. "Where did you get it?"

"From my..." She frowned, rubbing her head where he had struck her. "From a witch I'm journeying toward. She said it was for protection. I didn't think it would work this well," she added with a shaky laugh.

She sat up straighter in the nest, eyeing him with suspicion. She was smiling, which was strange. Wick had never had a mortal smile at him before. It looked nice on her, even when it flickered at the edges. Even if she still stank of fear.

"You didn't eat me," she said warily.

"No," Wick agreed.

"You begged me to hurt you. So I could..." Her smile got huge, like she was telling herself a satisfying joke. "So I could get away!"

"I do not want to kill if I do not have to," Wick said.

Briar laughed again. It was beginning to sound hysterical. Then she coughed, shaking her hair out of her face.

"Where are my manners?" she said, surprisingly casual as she tucked her knife into a belt holster. "I'm Briar Copperwood, notorious scamp and down-on-her-luck thief."

She held out her hand. Wick stared at it, uncomprehending. Was he meant to spit on it? He had seen humans spit on each other once. Then again, they hadn't looked very happy about it. Maybe that was an angry greeting, not a civil one.

He wanted very badly to be civil. He had not gotten

many chances. Most mortals he encountered met with an ugly end, unless he stayed at a safe distance. This was the closest he'd ever been to one without ripping them apart.

"I am Wick," said Wick. He didn't spit, just to be safe.

Briar reached out like she was going to touch his arm. Then her hand faltered and fell back to her belt, rubbing her dagger hilt.

"Nice to meet you, Wick," Briar said, laughing once more. "Never thought I'd say that to a Skullstalker. Void take me, I never thought I'd say anything to a Skullstalker except—OW!"

At first, he assumed it was part of her sentence. Then she jerked, her hands clasping her chest, and an agonized sound escaped from behind her teeth.

Wick stood, his horns scraping the top of the cave. "What is it?"

"Shit." She grimaced, her face twisting up before it forcibly smoothed out. "I need to get back to town—"

She cut off in another agonized cry, curling over in his nest. She smelled like pain and fire and death.

Wick fell to his knees beside her helplessly. He had always wanted to speak to a human like this, have a *real* conversation. Now it was finally happening, and she was dying because of... what?

"I do not understand what's happening," he told her.

She groaned, her knuckles becoming white where they clutched her chest.

"None of your business, big boy," she panted.

He bent down and inhaled. "You are dying. I smell no wound."

She choked out another laugh. This one was wet, the scent of salt joining the acrid stench of heat and death that was filling his cave.

"I do not understand," he repeated with increasing urgency.

Briar made an animal noise through her blunt teeth. "I'm cursed. Alright? Some entitled warlock *bastard* cursed me so that I—so that—" She swallowed, her expression collapsing in on itself. "I have to fuck someone every day, alright? Or I'll die. And the day's almost gone. I can feel it climbing my heart."

He sniffed harder. The stench of heat was creeping around her heart, getting hotter and hotter. It would be an unpleasant way to die.

Briar cried out and curled in on herself, shuddering.

Wick stepped back on instinct. His presence had never helped mortals, only hurt. But an idea was starting to brew in his mind, dubious and incredulous.

"I could help," he said.

She stared up at him, pained tears in her eyes. "What?"

Then she blinked, and her mouth opened in shock. She sat up again, shaking with effort as she considered him.

"Gods," she said. "I didn't even... But I guess you *do* have..."

She trailed off, her gaze dropping to his loincloth.

Then she jerked, squeezing her hands over her chest yet again.

"Shit," she hissed. "Are you serious?"

"Yes," he said, unable to keep the uncertainty out of his voice. He had never lain with anyone, mortal or otherwise. Any time he had come close, the blood frenzy took over. It was upsetting, and he quickly accepted that it was unavailable to him. But if she had that enchanted amulet, maybe it could work. And if the blood frenzy set in...

Well. She would die anyway. Hopefully, he would make it quicker than her curse.

Briar straightened again, pushing her sweaty hair out of her face. The cave was dim, but he could see her perfectly: her cheeks flushed with blood, her smile blazing despite the pain.

She looked almost... excited. The scent of excitement filled the cave, musky and hot. It was nice. Much nicer than cold, pungent fear that would most likely make him give in to the blood frenzy again.

"Fuck it," Briar whispered. "Let's go, big boy."

THREE

Briar half-expected him to pounce on her.

True, he hadn't eaten her yet. But he was still a Skullstalker. They were not known for their *lack* of appetite. If they wanted something, they would grab it.

But he didn't grab her. There was no pouncing. He only knelt there, so huge his bulk blocked out the moonlight streaming in from the mouth of the cave.

Briar frowned. *Is he waiting for me?* It seemed an incredibly polite thing to do, especially for a monster like him. Maybe Skullstalkers didn't have sexual urges like humans. Maybe—

Before she could ponder his urges anymore, another rush of pain swarmed over her and made her cry out.

Wick straightened, his ears pricking up in concern. "Briar?"

"We better get this show on the road," Briar said, gritting her teeth in a smile. "What are you waiting for, big boy?"

He did not make any acknowledgment of the nickname. Nor did he react when she placed her hand on his strange, pale chest, the highest part of him she could reach.

She shivered. His skin was so cold. But it would have to do if she wanted to survive another day.

She slid a hand down his belly until she reached his loincloth. Still, he did not move, staring down at her with those odd fiery eyes. She could only see half of his face under the skull mask, but she got the feeling he was out of his depth.

She gave him the best smile she could manage despite the pain. "I was kind of expecting you to ravish me, Wick. Time's a-wasting."

"Oh," said Wick, as if just remembering what they were doing. "Yes."

Then his hands were on her, so huge they encompassed her whole waist. Briar let out a gasp as he dragged her onto her back. The nest was shockingly comfortable. A few feathers poked into her sides, but the fur was heavenly.

He tugged at her belt with a confused frown. It took her a moment to realize what he was confused about.

"Buckle," she explained, working at it. She would have laughed if she wasn't stuck between fear and pain— she was lying under a Skullstalker, explaining what a belt buckle was so he could get her pants off and *fuck* her.

She fought down a wave of nerves as she slipped her

shoes off, then her pants. She'd been with some shady characters since the curse—voids, even *before* it—but she'd always done her best to make things as good as they could be. Which was fine if he were some drunk who could hardly get it up and was having her out the back of some grimy tavern. But it was trickier when he was a literal *monster*, looming over her with those huge fangs and claws.

At least he had a nice mouth. Even with the skull mask above it and the fangs inside it, his mouth was rather beautiful.

"Okay," Briar said, her voice higher than she intended. "Let me see what we're working with."

Wick, at least, understood that. He tugged at his loincloth. It pooled around his knees, and Briar's mouth fell open.

With shock, of course. But also, with a surprising amount of lust. He was massive, even half-hard, and he was... *mostly* human. There were a set of thick ridges circling his cock, which perked up under her gaze.

"Wow," Briar said faintly.

Wick grunted. "I am small for a Skullstalker. I... *should* be able to fit."

"I guess we'll find out," Briar said, instead of what she really wanted to say, which was *You're SMALL? What the fuck do BIG Skullstalkers look like? And why do you sound so unsure?*

She tensed against the nest, a pained shudder working through her body. It was almost to her heart; they were running out of time.

"Look," she said. "I know we're on a time limit, but I can't fit that inside me without some warming up."

"Oh," Wick said. He paused. Then he reached up and started to rub her arms uncertainly.

Briar laughed so loud it made them both jump. She kept expecting him to go feral on her, whether he wanted to or not. To show her this "blood frenzy" he had mentioned. But he acted like some city gentleman who had never been alone in a room with a woman. She had met many of the sort, usually before stealing something important and slipping out of their lives for good.

She never stayed long enough to get attached. It was better that she kept her heart to herself.

"Not like that. Warming up, like..." She eyed his pretty mouth dubiously. "I would get you to eat me out, but I don't love the look of those fangs."

"Eat you... *out*," Wick repeated, confused.

It made her wonder just how crude Skullstalker mating was. Did they not even go down on each other? How awful.

"With your tongue," she explained. "Inside me. But since you have those fangs—"

She cut off with a yelp as he leaned down and opened her legs. There was a moment when he just sat there, staring at her folds. Then he spread them with two huge fingers—Briar twitched with relief when she realized he could retract his claws—and rolled his tongue into her, huge and long and pink.

Briar yelled, grabbing his horns. She'd never felt

something like this before. And by the shocked rumble that Wick made, neither had he.

He pressed closer, nuzzling into her. The barest hint of fangs brushed her folds. The bottom of his skull mask grazed her clit.

Briar jerked. Another incredulous giggle spilled out of her. The fiery curse-pain was still there, but his tongue was a wonderful distraction. However, nothing would be a good distraction if the pain finally reached her heart.

Wick dragged her closer, his fangs bumping against her skin once more.

Briar shuddered. She was scared—how could she *not* be scared with a Skullstalker between her legs? But she had bigger things to worry about. Namely, getting herself loose enough to take his monstrous cock.

She threw her head back, focusing on the pleasure to try to speed up the process. His tongue was so far inside, working her open. She squeezed his horns, shocked to realize that she could actually come like this. While she tried to make sure she had a good time, she didn't always come these days. Survival mattered most.

Briar reached down to rub her clit. That telltale feeling was building in her stomach, ready to release.

Wick growled. The vibrations were what finally did her in, sending a thrilling buzz through her core.

"I'm going to come," she warned.

He made another low, delicious grumble. His grip tightened around her waist, holding her down against the nest.

Briar cried out, her legs locking over his shoulders as

she came. It washed over her in pulsing waves, growing stronger with each thrust of his tongue.

Wick's growl grew louder. He shoved his face harder against her, and Briar jolted as his fangs pressed against her hard enough to sting. The orgasm was fading, the fear creeping back as she felt his fangs.

"Okay, that's enough," Briar warned him.

Wick made another rumbling noise and pulled back. His chin was slick with her wetness, his huge tongue lapping up a sticky trail on her thigh before pulling back.

"You taste good," he rasped.

Briar shivered. The fire in his strange black eyes was swelling, just like the curse around her heart. *Fleeing from a flame only to get saved by a flame,* she thought nonsensically.

Wick nosed at her knee, his skull mask pressing into her skin. "Are you warm enough?"

Pain raced through Briar's ribs. She bit her tongue to stop another cry of pain. It didn't matter if she was loose enough; she was out of time.

"Lie down," she gasped.

Wick blinked. She pushed at his chest, feeling the soft give of cold, pale skin over his muscles. It took a moment before Wick moved to comply, lying down on his back in the nest with his wings splayed out over the nest.

Briar crawled over him. She actually preferred other positions, but she was *not* about to let a Skullstalker be the one in control right now.

She was still shocked he was giving her this much. Every time he moved, she expected him to push her to the nest and rut her like an animal. Which was... surprisingly hot, now that she thought about it. But it was the kind of hot that was better in dreams than reality. Right now, she was in pain and trying very hard not to be scared, even as her legs shook with aftershocks.

Wick only moved to place his hands on her hips. He was staring up at her, his mouth slack and stained with her juices. If Briar didn't know any better, she would say he looked amazed.

"Stay," she told him.

After a moment, Wick nodded.

She knelt on his legs and eyed the big, thick cock standing proudly between them. He was even bigger now that he was fully hard. The ridges around his width had grown rosy in a way that made her mouth water.

Briar ignored it. This was no time for ambitious blowjobs. She was on a time limit.

She braced herself over his length. Another rush of burning pain surged around her heart, so intensely she could barely stay kneeling.

Wick steadied her. "You smell worse."

"I'm fine," she assured him, shaking with pain. It was now or never.

She took a calming breath and positioned his cockhead at her entrance. Then she started to sink down.

It was a *stretch*. It took multiple thrusts for her to even fit the cockhead, and by the time it finally popped in, they were both moaning.

Well, *she* was moaning. Wick was making a low, guttural growl that should have made her skin crawl.

Instead, it made her feel... wanted. Which was not a feeling she was unused to. She had actually grown tired of it. But the idea that he was growling like that, those clawed hands twitching against her hips, so obviously affected, and yet he was staying still just like she asked...

It might have been enough for her to trust him if he were human.

The hot pain was receding. Not dissipating—not yet. But it was draining away the more she rode him.

Briar rolled her hips. His cock slipped deeper inside, bumping against his first ridge. She rocked down again, and they both gasped as the ridge sank into her.

She rode him faster. That ridge felt so good popping in and out of her, she almost forgot about what she had to do. She had to make this monster come inside her before the day ticked over.

She leaned over him, staring into his fiery eyes. "How does it feel, big boy? Do I feel good?"

Wick made a strangled roar. His hips spasmed, his claws pressing into her hips.

"You feel," he started, his voice so thick it was barely recognizable. "You smell like— You're so—"

He cut off with a guttural growl. His horns shoved against the nest, his wings shuddering under him.

Briar rode him faster. It was always more difficult when she let herself get swept away like this, but she had a job to do: not die. And she wasn't going to get distracted just because of the pleasure jolting through her every time she bounced on his dick ridges.

"So big," she moaned. "Feels so good."

She was pulling out all her usual lines, but for once, she didn't have to fake it. Her moans were short and shocked, none of the high, airy ones she usually made to make men come faster. The deeper she sat on his cock, the harder it was to perform for him.

She unlaced her shirt, kneading her breasts. "Touch me. I need you."

Wick groaned, wings shuddering against the nest. He reached up with one shaky hand to squeeze her breasts, pulling at the nipples like she had just been doing. His claws were so gentle. Every touch made her heart beat faster. He could push her down at any time, could tear her to shreds, and yet he was being so careful to make it good for her.

"Just like that," she encouraged.

His hips jerked up, forcing his cock impossibly deep.

Briar yelled. She was getting close again; she could feel it. And the closer she got, the more she wanted him to disobey her rules. To shove him over onto her hands and knees and *take* her, the way she wanted to be taken. The way she never let anybody take her. She wanted his hot breath in her ear, his strong arms around her body as he plowed into her. She wanted those spiked wings looming over her, those growls getting louder and louder as he fucked deeper inside.

Wick's hips jumped again. He was fucking her properly now, and Briar knew she should warn him to stay still like she'd asked. But she was opening up so sweetly around him, a second ridge popping inside as she sank deeper. It felt so good that she let him keep doing it.

He dropped her breasts, his hands wrapping around her waist. He pulled her down with each thrust, and Briar wailed as he used her body. Usually, it triggered a series of dirty feelings she had to ignore to enjoy things. But it was hard to feel anything but pure pleasure as he shoved his ridged cock deeper and deeper.

Briar whimpered, bracing her hands on his chest as he lifted her, pulling her back down on his cock.

Wick's growl grew louder. The fire in his eyes swelled until she could feel the heat on her face as he stared hungrily up at her.

It wasn't just lust, she realized with a jolt. This was *blood* hunger.

But before the fear could truly take hold, her necklace glowed.

Briar looked down. The necklace bounced between her breasts with each thrust. White light filled the cave, washing them both in a pale glow.

Wick's thrusts faltered. His hands loosened around her waist, his claws retracting where they were almost breaking the skin. The fire in his eyes dimmed, a shocked noise spilling out of his throat.

"Briar," he rasped urgently.

He was going to ask if she was okay. She could tell. But she couldn't handle that kind of sweetness, even from a Skullstalker. Despite all her efforts, she still had an unbearably soft heart. She wasn't about to let an unnaturally kind monster near it.

"Big boy," she replied, rolling her hips as fast as she

could, breath hitching on every pass of those gorgeous ridges. "D-do me a favor and come for me, will you?"

She squeezed her inner walls around him. It took tremendous effort, given how stretched she was around him. But it apparently worked because he threw back his head and let out a ragged roar that made her heart skip a beat.

He gripped her hips bruisingly tight, holding her still as he emptied inside her. Briar's mouth fell open as she felt him pulse, his spend coating her insides.

It felt incredible. But more importantly, the curse-fire was leaking away from her chest.

She was safe for another day. And just in time.

She sagged over him, bracing herself on wobbly elbows. His chest was so broad she could rest on it easily.

For a moment, there was no sound in the cave but their heavy breathing. She trembled against him, her body racing with the aftermath of pleasure and the relief of living another day. It took her a moment to realize Wick was shaking, too.

She eased up, wincing as his soft cock slipped out of her. They hadn't fit his whole cock inside, but they had gotten pretty damn close.

"Thanks," she panted. "I can't believe a Skullstalker just saved my life."

Wick made a low, gurgling growl. He let go of her hips, digging instead into the nest. His claws flexed in the furs and pierced the thick hide like a knife through butter.

Briar giggled weakly and lay down on his chest. She

meant to climb off and gather up her clothes, like she did after every coupling since she had been cursed. But she was so tired after the strange, exciting turn the night had taken, and the Skullstalker's heart was beating so slowly under her cheek, like a lullaby.

Briar's eyes drifted reluctantly shut. She would get up in a minute.

The last thing she felt before she fell asleep was a pair of huge arms closing hesitantly around her.

Four

Wick woke up panicked.

At first, he didn't know why. Then he felt something small and warm shifting in his arms, an unfamiliar scent washing over him.

Wick looked down. The strange human from last night was dozing against his chest.

He sniffed her carefully, pulling her back to examine her naked body.

No blood. No scent of pain in the air. The amulet around her neck had worked its strange magic: he had not hurt her during the night.

Wick slumped with relief. He gathered her back in his arms, setting her cheek against his chest once again. She hummed, nuzzling against him.

Wick touched her hair, charmed. No one had ever touched him like this before. His encounters with other creatures were brief and bloody, and that was only when he couldn't avoid them entirely. He sometimes talked to his brothers, but that was rare. When they did talk, they never touched unless it was to try to rip his throat out.

He had watched humans do this from a distance, once. A young couple curled together on a blanket, sweat cooling on their naked bodies. He had watched them through the trees until the blood frenzy started to itch under his skin, then he fled. But he hadn't been able to shake that image from his head. How gently they'd held each other.

He rubbed a cautious hand down Briar's bare back. It was even softer than he dreamed.

He stroked Briar's cheek next. She was curled up against him with her limbs bunched tight against her body, like she was prepared to leap up and flee at any moment. She had scars decorating her body—knife marks and burn marks and other marks he didn't recognize. Some of them looked several decades old. Or perhaps mortals' scars aged differently from Skull-stalkers'.

Briar stirred against him. Her body was so warm. Her thighs were covered with his dried come.

He buried his face in her hair and inhaled. Sweet with sleep and salty with his spend, it was such an intoxicating combination of scents he could feel himself getting hard again.

He looked down at his cock, filling out against his thigh. The ridges stiffened with it, flushing the same color as his cockhead. She had seemed especially eager whenever he fit those ridges into her. After the shock faded, anyhow. At the start, she had been so surprised it made him wonder if she'd slept with a man with a ridged cock before. Surely, she must. If she had to sleep with someone every day, she had to have run into a man with a ridged cock. Skullstalkers had a variety of cocks, human men must be the same.

Briar shifted. He glanced at her, curled so tightly against him, then down at his cock. He was still surprised how much had fit inside her. He *was* smaller than his brothers, but not by much. His older brother Slate had needed a magic spell for him to fit inside his wife.

A gurgling sound echoed around the cave. Wick startled, only to realize that it had come from Briar's stomach.

Humans needed to eat more often than Skullstalkers, Wick remembered. Slate had experienced this very problem when he encountered his new wife. He had tried asking Wick about what humans ate, and Wick had given his best approximation of a mortal diet, only for Slate to realize that Wick was talking out of his tail. Wick had never been around mortals long enough to know what they ate.

But he had a vague memory of Slate mentioning something about eggs.

She was still asleep when he got back to the cave. For a moment, he just stood there and watched her, curled up in the morning light with her limbs tucked in like she was protecting herself against something.

Maybe she was cold. Slate had mentioned that mortals felt the temperature more than Skullstalkers.

Wick took a step toward her clothes, which were in a pile next to her. A twig snapped under his foot.

Briar sat up so fast he thought she had been lying in wait. Then she blinked groggily, and Wick realized that she had just woken up that quickly.

She looked up at him, startled. "*Gods*!"

Wick raised the hand that wasn't holding an egg. "Hello."

Briar laughed and sat up, pulling her knees up to cover her nakedness. For a moment, she looked almost shy. Then she grinned, her cheeks flushing.

"So, it wasn't a dream," she said. Then she shifted and winced. "*Definitely* not a dream. Ow."

"Ow?" Wick sniffed the air. Still no blood. "I hurt you?"

"Only the good kind of hurt, big boy." She closed one eye at him.

Wick frowned. The eye-gesture seemed significant, but he didn't understand what it meant. She was smiling, so he assumed she meant it to be good.

"I didn't mean to," he tried.

Her smile faltered. Then it came back, bigger but somehow paler than before.

"You *are* a big boy. Couldn't be helped." She hugged her knees, resting her chin on them. "And it wasn't like I didn't have a good time. You enjoyed yourself, right?"

It was probably the best night of Wick's life.

"Yes," he said honestly.

"Lovely!" Briar ran a hand through her hair, glancing up at him. No, glancing *around* him.

Toward the cave opening.

He paused. She didn't smell like fear, but she didn't look completely at ease. If she wanted to leave, he wasn't going to stop her. He just needed to ask her something first.

"Well," Briar said. "I should..."

Then she stopped, squinting at him. "Are you... holding an egg?"

"What? Oh." He looked down at the egg in his hand. "Yes. I collected two, but the second broke on the way back down the tree."

He held out the remaining egg.

Briar stared at it. Her smile was getting smaller, but the discomfort was gone from her face.

Wick looked at the egg consideringly. "Is it not suitable?"

"No, no! It's great!" Briar took the egg, examining it with a grin. "Haven't done this in ages."

She cracked it into her open mouth and swallowed it with a grimace.

"Better than nothing," she announced.

Wick had the feeling he had done something wrong. "Are eggs undesirable for mortals?"

"No!" Briar said, wiping her mouth. "We just usually cook it first."

"Oh." Wick cursed himself silently. Slate had mentioned mortals and their tendency to cook everything.

Mortals and their blunt teeth, Slate had told him of his wife. *Their sharpest ones couldn't tear into a newborn rabbit. They even need to cook plants.*

He didn't understand why she had an issue with eggs. A raw egg seemed to go down easily enough. But it was clear that he knew even less about mortals than he thought he did.

Wick sat down at the other end of the nest. He had never realized how small it was until now, their knees almost touching despite his best attempts. He'd never had anyone in his nest before.

"You are traveling to the witch who gave you that amulet," Wick said.

Briar touched it curiously. "I am."

Wick paused. His older brother Slate was always telling him to be fiercer. Fewer questions, more demands.

"I will go with you," he said confidently.

Briar startled. "You'll *what*?"

He gestured at the amulet hanging between her breasts. "If she made that amulet, she might know how to cure me. *Truly* cure me."

He could hardly let himself hope. He had been to magic users of all kinds—even a fellow Skullstalker. And they all said the same thing: he was beyond hope. The blood frenzy was as deep in him as his bones.

"I can protect you," he offered. "No one will hurt you when I am around. And I can help you with your curse."

Briar stared at him. She shifted on the spot, and

Wick's nose twitched under his skull mask as he smelled the dried come on her thighs.

Then Briar burst out into laughter, curling over with the force of it.

"Sorry," she gasped. Her cheeks were suddenly salty, and Wick frowned before he realized she smelled like giddy shock. Apparently, humans cried at strange times.

Her laughter trailed off into giggles. She wiped her tears away with the back of her hand.

"I *did* mean to find a man to accompany me through the forest," Briar said, still chuckling. "You know what? Sure. A down-on-her-luck thief and her gentleman Skull-stalker guard."

"Wick," he reminded her. He didn't know how reliable human memory was.

"Wick," she repeated, like she was surprised by it. She gave him an evaluating look, hidden quickly with another blazing smile.

"Well then. Time's a-wasting." She eased herself to her feet, gloriously bare. Then she took a step and winced. "Wow. That will be... an *adjustment*, if we have to do that every night."

"I can just use the tip," Wick offered. "If that is easier for you."

Her brows rose. A pretty flush covered her cheeks, and Wick's mouth watered.

Briar averted her eyes with another nervous laugh. "We'll see what happens," she said, bending to pick up her pants off the nest's floor.

Wick watched her dress. He had a vague inkling that

he should help—he had watched a mortal man do that for a woman once—but that was for a dress, which looked infinitely more complicated. Not to mention, he had no clue how to work those "buckles," nor the laces on her shirt.

She pulled the laces closed over her breasts and turned to him. "Good as new. Do we need to do anything before we leave? Water any plants? Lock the door on the way out?"

Wick looked around the cave. He only had his nest. Plus a stack of shiny rocks in the corner that he liked to collect. But he could leave them here. Wherever he went, there were usually nicer rocks.

"No," he said simply. "Do we need to lie together? Or should we wait until the sun goes down?"

Briar shifted from foot to foot, considering. Wick tried to focus on the pain she had shown before and not the sudden ache under his loincloth. He had never felt anything as good as Briar's hole fluttering around him, trying to take him deeper.

"Let's give a lady time to recover," Briar said finally. She closed one eye at him again.

Wick nodded and wondered if this was a good time to ask about the eye-closing thing. It was obviously significant.

He led her out of the cave. Briar seemed eager to step out into the forest, her shoulders sagging in relief as the sunlight fell on her skin. Then she spotted the dead human from last night and huffed.

"Good riddance," she said softly.

Wick looked over at her. Based on her attitude before, he had expected her to be more dismissive, or even victorious over his death. But she sounded almost regretful as they walked away from him, deeper into the forest.

"Did you know him?" Wick asked.

"Who?" Briar twisted to look at the corpse behind them in surprise. "Oh, him? Barely. He's a bounty hunter. At least, he is *now*. Apparently, some of my fellow thieves, criminals, and bandits came together to hunt me down. That's why I was in your cave in the first place; I needed something big and bad to distract them while I ran."

It was a sensible tactic. Wick didn't know why it made his chest feel heavy.

"Bounty hunter?" he asked.

She frowned up at him, uncomprehending. She looked different in the daylight, her features thrown into stark relief. She looked... weary. Like she was older than her years. From the little he knew of humans, she was in her younger adult years. But she carried herself like she had seen much of the world and its dangers.

"Oh," she said, her brow smoothing with understanding. "A bounty hunter is someone who collects someone for money. Usually dead. You don't get out much, do you?"

"Not often," he agreed.

She cocked her head at him, considering. Her pale hair fell over her face, and Wick experienced the strange sensation of wanting to push it behind her ears. It was the same impulse that made him want to pat baby rabbits and stroke river moss. It was usually followed by blood and claw marks.

Wick clenched his hands into fists. The blood frenzy was dormant, for now. But never for long.

"I thought Skullstalkers lived in voids," she said thoughtfully.

"Not me," he admitted. "I've always lived in the mortal realm."

"Really? Huh." Briar craned her head, frowning through the trees. "Gods, it's going to take forever to get to Marigold's place from here."

"Marigold?"

"The witch." Briar paused, looking up at him thoughtfully. She stepped in front of him, bringing them both to a stop.

"What is it?" Wick asked.

Briar reached up and, with only a little hesitation, touched a spike on the edge of his wing. "These things work, right?"

"They do," Wick said slowly, confused. She had seen him fly briefly last night; he remembered flying at the bounty hunters, though his memories were spotty with blood frenzy.

Briar smiled pointedly up at him.

"You want me to fly," he realized. "But what about you?"

She laughed. Then, when she noticed he wasn't joking, she touched his wing with both hands.

"You're strong enough to carry one little ol' thief," she said.

Wick stopped. She meant for him to... *carry* her? It made sense, now that he thought about it. He just had never done it before. Even the idea made him nervous. She could fall from his arms, or the amulet could fall from her neck, causing him to go into a blood frenzy all the way up in the air.

"Just an idea," she said with a placating smile. "If that's not your style, then—oh gods!"

She cut off with a bright laugh as he hefted her into his arms. She was inconsequentially light, just as she was last night. He worried he would frighten her, or that he should have warned her first. But the fear coming from her skin was so faint he almost didn't notice it.

"Alright then," she said, wriggling against his chest. "Let's go, big boy."

Five

Flying in a Skullstalker's arms was by far Briar's favorite near-death experience.

Even with the ground looming a deadly distance away and a literal monster breathing down her neck, she couldn't help the wild grin that spread over her face, which ached after what must have been at least an hour in the air.

They were covering so much ground! At this rate, they would make it to Marigold's cottage in *days*, not weeks.

"Woo-hoo," Briar yelled, the noise getting caught in the cool spring wind. "I'm *flying*!"

"You keep yelling that," Wick said. Then he sniffed her. "You smell strange. Fearful, but also very happy."

Briar twisted to stare at him. His fiery eyes were fixed on the trees below, scanning for gods knew what.

"You can *smell* that?" Briar demanded.

Wick made a distracted rumbling noise. Then he

blinked, his fiery eyes fixing on her. Not for the first time, Briar was astounded by them. Not just the flames, but the fact that there was no danger in them. She had been looked at with malice so often that it was strange to be under his soft, curious gaze.

"I have a keen nose," was all he said.

Briar huffed a laugh into his chest, hoping he couldn't smell her worries. She based her entire life around tricking people; she couldn't have some monster sniffing her out.

"Is that a Skullstalker thing?" she asked.

He made another rumbling noise. He sounded like an old dog, and Briar had to fight back a shocking wave of affection. This wasn't a cute old spaniel sitting at the back of a tea shop. This was a *Skullstalker*. Even if he was helping her, he was still a monster. If she didn't have Marigold's amulet, he would have ripped her to shreds last night.

Her stomach gurgled. She grimaced. That egg hadn't lasted very long. It didn't help that she hadn't had dinner last night.

Wick frowned. "You are hungry again?"

"I can last," she assured him.

But Wick was already flying down toward the trees.

"I *said* I can last," she complained as they headed for the treetops.

"My wings are growing tired," Wick said. "This will be a welcome rest."

Briar narrowed her eyes as he weaved through the trees with surprising delicateness and landed gently on the ground, still holding her like he didn't quite know what to do next.

"What will you eat?" he asked. "I can find another bird nest. I will be more careful with the eggs this time."

"Thanks," she said, easing herself out of his grip and landing on her feet. "But I was thinking of something more substantial."

"Substantial?"

Briar looked around, considering. There was enough around for her to construct a shoddy trap.

"Like a squirrel," she started.

Wick nodded determinedly and took off.

"Wait," she called after him. "I didn't mean—"

But he was already flying off, looking determinedly through the trees.

"—you," she finished.

Wick ignored her. He hovered in midair for a moment, then sped up a tree so fast that Briar jumped. There was an animal shriek and a small *pop*, and Wick turned to her with a dead squirrel hanging from his claws.

"Found one," he announced.

He flew down, his movements oddly stiff like he was holding himself back.

The amulet glowed around Briar's neck. The closer Wick got, the smoother his movements became.

Briar closed her hand around the glowing amulet. He was holding himself back from a frenzy, she realized, most likely triggered by killing the squirrel. If she didn't have the amulet...

Wick landed in front of her, shaking his shoulders like he was shaking off a bad thought.

"Here." He held the squirrel out uncertainly, much like he had held out the egg.

She took it. Then she stared at him until it clicked.

"Oh," he said. "Cooking."

Briar patted his chest. It wasn't as cold as it was last night. *Probably because I've been cuddled against his chest for the last hour,* she thought.

"I'll take care of this part," she assured him.

An admirably short time later, Briar had the rabbit skinned and rotating over a makeshift spit.

"Are you sure you don't want any?" she asked as she turned the stick.

"I do not hunger as mortals do. I will not need to feed for..." Wick paused to consider this. "Perhaps a week."

"Really?" That went against every bedtime story she'd heard about Skullstalkers. "I heard you guys were ravenous. You know, eternal hunger, cursed to roam the land feeding on whatever was unfortunate enough to stumble into your lair."

Wick stared at her. "*You* stumbled into my lair. I did not feed on you."

"Only because I got lucky." She flicked the amulet around her neck, and they both watched it settle against her collarbones.

She meant it to be a joke. But Wick didn't smile as he averted his gaze.

"Mortals do not know much about our kind."

You don't know much about mortals, either, Briar thought. He didn't even know what they *ate*. He'd been living in the mortal realm for his entire existence—however long that was—and he still didn't know basic facts about mortals. It must have been a very secluded existence. Or maybe he was spending time with other Skullstalkers. Briar had been told they were a solitary bunch, but what did she know?

Wick shifted in the dirt. He was sitting across from her, holding his knees like she had done in the cave this morning. Almost like he was trying to make himself smaller, Briar thought with amusement. He didn't want to intimidate her. It was... sweet. Even if half his face was a skull, and he could rip her apart with one claw.

"So," he said as rabbit fat dripped onto the fire below, throwing sparks. "Why were you being hunted?"

Briar made sure her smile was still in place. She hadn't actually had to explain her situation to anybody yet. They either already knew, and she didn't have to say a word, or they didn't know, and she wanted to keep it that way. This curse was just another string of bad luck that Briar would do her best to forget about as soon as it was over.

No looking back. It was the only way to get through a life like hers. Do anything else, and you would go mad with pain and bitterness.

"The warlock who cursed me had a rich family," she

explained. "Not that it did me any good. I didn't even get to rob him after I hacked his head off."

Wick grunted. Briar watched him carefully. Most common folk didn't like thieves. But Wick was hardly common folk.

"You desire riches," Wick said finally.

Briar laughed. She was tempted to leave it there and let him believe what everybody else believed: that she was a greedy, black-hearted thief with a great rack. But who was he going to tell if she was truthful for once?

"I want *comfort*," she corrected him. "You know. Food on the table. Warm place to sleep every night. Nobody knocking down my door asking for a fight. Money means I can have those things."

"I have no money," Wick pointed out. "I have comfort."

Briar snorted. That nest *was* pretty comfortable. She'd had pretty dreams last night, all sweetness and softness. She'd woken once to find herself swaddled in Wick's huge arms and wasn't even aware enough to struggle out of them. She'd drifted back to sleep full of a safety that only existed in her far-fetched dreams.

"I would have more," Wick continued, watching rabbit fat drip into the flames. "If I could control myself."

Briar toyed with the amulet using the hand that wasn't turning the spit. "Speaking of control. What's with your *blood frenzy*, anyway? I've never heard of that."

"Then you are like all else I have spoken to," Wick said. "I have memories of fighting. My brother insists they're dreams; he says any wars Skullstalkers fought were won long before we were born."

Briar had no knowledge of *any* wars involving Skullstalkers. She didn't know Skullstalkers dreamed. She didn't know Skullstalkers had siblings. It was an oddly cute idea.

"Your brother?"

"Slate," Wick explained. "Mortals know him as the Bygone. He rules the wanderer's void."

Briar hadn't been warned of the Bygone since she lived on the other side of the country. As far as she knew, he was a fairy story to stop travelers from stepping off forest paths.

Wick sighed, his tail flicking distractedly behind him. "I wish I could speak with him. He could get us to your witch's place with a portal."

"A portal," Briar repeated. "Since when can Skullstalkers make portals?"

"He is very old and very powerful," Wick replied. He gripped his tail, stroking it absentmindedly. "I am not good at magic. Only killing."

He sounded sad about it. He was obviously trying to hide it, but Briar was well-versed in seeing past the emotional facades of men. Even if they were Skullstalker men. And Wick was surprisingly easy to read, for someone who had a motionless skull for half his face. His fiery eyes narrowed and contracted, his wings and tail twitched, and his body language might as well have been verbal for how helpful it was in spelling out how he was feeling.

Which, as far as Briar could tell, was deeply awkward.

Briar leaned over the campfire to pat his arm. "Well, at least you feel bad about it."

Wick blinked at her hand. Briar leaned back and continued turning the spit, ignoring how her hand was tingling. She'd spent a long time pressed up against this monster, never mind that she was unconscious for most of it. There was no reason for the thrill that ran through her at the feel of his cool skin.

"So," she said. "Say this works. My friend lifts your blood curse using whatever magic she used to fuel my protection necklace. What are you going to do?"

"I don't know," Wick admitted. "It is not as if I can live in a town. Mortals do not like Skullstalkers, and I am not suited to crowds. I suppose I would find somewhere quiet, like I always do. But I would venture wherever I wished and know that I would only attack if I wished it."

You would have to attack everywhere you went, Briar thought to herself. *People would ambush you on sight.*

Still, it was an admirable ambition. It was actually shockingly close to hers, if she thought about it.

"That sounds peaceful," she admitted.

"That is all I want," Wick replied. "Peace."

He tipped his head up to the sky. Watching the birds, Briar thought. Or maybe watching the sunlight through the branches.

Do not get attached to the Skullstalker, Briar told herself sternly. She had been very good at not getting attached. It only brought pain and regret. She was not going to break a good streak just because some monster wanted to settle down sometime.

She pulled up a lazy grin. "So, what, you'd buy a little cottage somewhere?"

"What? No. I only need my nest. Ideally, in a cave, or somewhere else secluded." Wick paused, cocking his head at a bird flying above the trees. "But perhaps a nest near a waterfall."

Do not get attached, Briar hissed to herself, even louder than last time.

She eased the rabbit off the spit and examined the hot flesh. "Maybe I can come and visit you when I'm rich!"

Wick looked surprised. "I would enjoy that. I... I have never had a friend before. Except my brother, I suppose."

Briar stopped, her mouth snapping shut before she could bite into the rabbit. She moved it out of the way to stare at him.

"You want to be friends," she said, only managing to make it sound funny on the last words, "With lil ol' me?"

"I do," said Wick.

As if it were that easy. As if Briar wasn't a husk of empty smiles wrapped in a lot of charm. As if she would ever be friends with someone who could kill her so easily. But his face was so damn earnest she actually had to hide how touched she was.

"Great," she said chirpily. "To friendship, big boy."

She tore off a steaming piece of rabbit and held it out. He sniffed it, bemused.

"Come on," she goaded.

"It smells strange."

"That's because it's cooked." She held it out further.

Wick ate it off her fingers. Briar held still, forcing herself not to shiver as that big, pink tongue licked rabbit fat off her palm.

"Hmmm." He sat back, flames twisting thoughtfully in his huge eyes. "It is... fine."

Briar couldn't help it: she laughed. Truly laughed, nothing fake about it. She tried to rein it in, as always. But he had heard much of her genuine laughter, even if most of it was hysterical.

She could allow true parts of herself to seep through with him. It wasn't like they would stick together after their journey finished. Even if he did get his heart's desire and live peacefully next to a waterfall, she would be too busy to visit him. Striving for the next heist, the next town, the next haul that would finally set her for life—not that any of them ever did. She was closer to forty than thirty now, and she was as broke and alone as ever.

She *did* want peace. But she doubted she'd ever get it. Void, the Skullstalker probably had a better chance at it than she did.

"Briar."

Briar blinked. Her name sounded odd in his mouth. She couldn't work out why. Probably the fangs.

"You smell sad," he continued.

Briar almost squished the freshly cooked rabbit. She let go of it fast, blowing on her overheated hands. Right, he could *smell* her emotions. She just had to keep a handle on them, make sure they didn't get too strong. Luckily, she had a lifetime of practice.

"I'm just worried," she said, which was not untrue. "I know I don't have to worry about the curse while you're here. But I don't know what I'll do if we get separated and I'm alone in the woods."

"We will not get separated," Wick said dismissively. He licked a stray shred of rabbit from his claws, and Briar's gaze fell once more to the pink length.

"There is nothing powerful enough to keep me from you," he continued, still licking. That long tongue curled around his entire wrist, sliding over a slick trail of rabbit fat.

Briar's breath caught in her chest. His tongue and his stupidly sweet words were making her clit throb. Since when was she attracted to that? His monstrous tongue should make her shudder, and not in anticipation. His words should make her laugh, as many men have made her laugh as they attempted to seduce her.

And yet, there was something enticing about it. His monstrous form combined with such softness. The knowledge that he had all that power and ferocity, and he didn't want to turn it on her.

She folded her legs tighter. Could he smell the wetness between her legs?

Wick's tongue slowed and stilled. His fiery eyes locked on her, and Briar cursed silently.

"Oh," Wick said. "Is it time?"

Six

Wick lay her down in the dirt and wished for fur.

It seemed... incorrect for her to be bare against the forest floor. Why, he didn't know. When he voiced this, Briar smiled at him so brightly that the crisp scent of her amusement burned through her stress.

"I should only lie in the finest silks," she said. "Thank you for noticing. Now, do get on with it."

She spread her legs wider, exposing that thick patch of hair between her legs. Her folds glistened, and Wick's mouth watered in response.

He lowered his head and licked a stripe up her thigh. She shuddered underneath him, her head tipping back.

"We can take our time," she told him. "We have ages."

It would probably be for the best. He genuinely needed to give his wings a rest. Wick had not realized how little he flew until he did it for a long stretch. Briar did not weigh much, but he was feeling her additional weight after that flight, his wings aching where they were folded against his back.

Wick rubbed his mouth against the coarse hair at the apex of her legs. Her skin pebbled under his touch. Her scent was intoxicating, if only there wasn't that note of fear underneath it. It was so small that Wick almost didn't notice it, but every once in a while, it would flare, bitter and unwanted.

He sat up. "You are still fearful."

Briar scoffed. For a moment, she was a flurry of contrasting emotions, all of them jumbling until he couldn't tell them apart. She looked ashamed, which made little sense. Then she smiled, and the shame was gone.

"I'm not scared," she insisted. "I just value my life. You're a trustworthy Skullstalker! But you're still a Skullstalker. And I don't trust easy. Alright?"

"I would never hurt you unless I lost myself," he reminded her. "And with your necklace, I will not."

He touched the necklace where it lay between her naked breasts. The amulet was as big as his claw, but no bigger. The sight reminded him to retract his claws, which he did with haste—Briar's skin was so breakable, after all.

He looked back up at her face. She was staring at him, her eyes wide and her expression unreadable.

Wick inhaled deeply. Her emotions were a confusing mix, and lust was only one of many.

"What is it?" he asked.

She shook her head. If he were only judging from her face, he would truly think nothing was wrong.

"Just not used to men being so worried about hurting me," she said, her smile twisting wryly. "Or women, for that matter. You know that dead warlock jackass cursed me, so it *had* to be a man who came in me? Very inconvenient."

"Very," Wick agreed, trying to work out how a woman could possibly come inside her. The list of things he didn't know about mortals was growing longer with every passing hour he spent with this strange mortal.

He licked between her legs again, his eyes falling shut in bliss as he tasted her for the second time. He had never tasted anything like it, heady and sweet and intoxicating.

Briar gasped, grabbing his horns. She smelled excited, the smell surrounding him as he pressed his tongue deeper.

Her folds parted around him as he pressed inside. She was tight, but she was slowly giving way, just as she had last night.

She tasted different. Saltier. More musk.

Me, Wick realized as he licked up his own come, still warm from last night. *She tastes like me.*

He licked eagerly, eating his spend out of her.

Briar moaned, lifting her legs onto his shoulders. "You know, I really thought I'd get eaten by a Skullstalker last night. I just didn't think it would be like—"

She cut off in a desperate moan as his tongue bumped a certain spot inside her. She arched against him, and Wick rubbed at the spot curiously with the tip of his tongue.

"Ohhhh *shit*," Briar said, her voice cracking. She was still grinning, her thighs shaking as she closed them tighter around his shoulders. "Right there, big boy."

Wick rumbled against her. Nobody had given him a title other than "brother." He liked being her big boy.

He thrust his tongue deeper, feeling her inner walls stretch. The delicious taste got headier the further he went, her wetness growing more copious. The air filled with the sound of their slickness. He was drooling, he could feel it dripping down her thighs and ass.

"Fuck," Briar whispered. "Do I taste good? You're making such a mess of me."

Wick growled and pressed closer. He wanted to bury his face against her, shove his tongue as far as it could go. He had never been hungry for another creature like this. It was so close to frenzy, except it didn't feel destructive. Instead of tearing something apart, he was bringing her pleasure. He had never made somebody smell like this before, all eagerness and excitement, the air so thick with it he could hardly tell it from his own.

Briar scraped her nails over the top of his skull mask where bone met skin, making him shiver. "I bet you're so h-hard right now. Never met anyone who wants to get their tongue in me like you. Sounds like you're gonna starve if you don't."

Mortals are fools if they do not long for this, Wick thought. He might be able to come from this alone if she told him to. He wanted nothing more than to stay here between her thighs and feel her spasm around his tongue; until he remembered how good she had felt around his cock.

Wick pulsed under his loincloth. He suddenly wanted nothing more than to hold her down and mount her, the urge old and deep, much like the blood frenzy. He forced it back. He might be a monster, but he was not without reason. He did not want her to be scared of him. He would mate her only how she wanted to be mated.

And it wasn't as if mating her with his tongue was a chore. His mouth watered longingly as he thrust his tongue deeper, last night's spend trickling out around his tongue.

"Yes," Briar breathed, her cheeks bright with ecstasy. "Eat it out of me. Gonna fill me up with a new load soon, huh? Will you eat it out of me every day?"

Yes, Wick thought desperately. He gripped her thighs as hard as he dared, taking care to keep his claws retracted as he plunged deeper and deeper. He made sure to graze that spot inside her that made her buck against him, slick coating his tongue. Soon she was writhing against the ground, her breath coming prey-fast.

"Oh," she whined, her eyes clenched shut and her muscles tense as her hips worked against him. "Oh, there, yes, *Wick*—"

She broke off in a triumphant cry and stilled, shaking. A flood of delicious slick gushed out around Wick's tongue, and he groaned as he lapped it up.

He worked her until Briar shuddered violently, pulling at his horns.

"C'mon," she breathed. "Get in me already. Stretched me out good, I can take it."

He pulled his tongue out reluctantly. There was a small, flushed nub at the top of her opening; she had been rubbing it last night, he remembered now.

He licked it curiously. Briar made a noise not unlike a sob, her whole body contracting.

Wick sat back, alarmed.

Briar grabbed his horn. "Feels good," she assured him. "Touch that when you're inside me, okay? *Gently*."

"Okay," Wick said. It was difficult to speak right now. Like his body was only made for grunts and roaring.

He climbed over her and untied his loincloth. He was dropping it to the forest floor when he smelled a sharp tinge of fear.

He looked down at Briar. She did not look distressed, and lust still hung thick in the air. But there was no mistaking that fear, acrid and stinging.

He was looming over her, he realized. It was probably unnerving to have a monster pinning you down like this.

"Sorry," he said, leaning back.

She caught his horn again. Her teeth dug into her lower lip, chest heaving as she considered.

Wick waited. "Briar?"

"It's okay," Briar said. "Just... give me a second."

She pushed him back enough for her to get on her hands and knees. The sight made Wick's heart thud in his chest, especially when she looked over her shoulder and closed one eye at him.

"Okay," she said. "Have at me."

She ground back against him. His cock twitched against her ass cheeks, and he forgot to be disappointed that he could no longer see her face.

He lined himself up against her lower hole, remembering how she had positioned herself last night. How long she had rocked herself on his cockhead before it had finally slipped inside.

He pressed in carefully. It took several passes for the cockhead to fit inside, after which he had to grip her hips and stop himself from shoving in as deep as he could, pressing all four ridges inside.

Slow, he reminded himself. *You do not want to hurt her.*

He thrusted shallowly, shaking with the effort of restraining himself. But her moans were so pretty, the scent of her lust clouding his head until his blood roared.

He pushed in further. The first ridge popped inside, and Briar cried out.

Wick squeezed her waist. "You enjoy that."

"I do!" Briar giggled, her mouth open as she panted. "N-never had a cock like this before."

Wick frowned. Apparently, he had been wrong about mortal cocks. "Mortals do not have ridges?"

"No," she said breathlessly. "Just Skullstalkers."

He wanted to mention that not all Skullstalkers had ridges. But then she was pushing back against him, and all thoughts flooded out of his mind except how good she felt around him.

He pushed deeper, fitting the second ridge into her tight hole.

Briar groaned. A drop of sweat rolled down her spine. He leaned down and licked it up, feeling her quake under his touch.

"*Oh*," she gasped, her eyelids fluttering each time his ridges caught on her hole. "Oh, oh, *ohhh*!"

She was not smiling anymore, her mouth twitching as if she would like to, but each thrust ruined her intention. Her hands clawed at the earth, a giddy laugh puffing out of her as he worked his cock into her, two ridges deep.

Wick growled, thrusting faster. He felt wild with it. The start of a blood frenzy flickered at the edges of his eyes.

Wait, he told himself, even as he sped up and his thoughts grew dim. *Don't—*

The amulet glowed. His thoughts were suddenly clearer. He could make himself slow down again, stop trying to push so deep. He was almost at his third ridge.

Briar arched, the curve of her spine so tantalizing he had to lick it again. The amulet was still glowing, washing the ground below her in white light.

"You're so deep," she told him as he curled his tongue over her neck. "*Gods*. How much is left?"

Wick leaned back to check. It was still hard to think, but at least with the amulet glowing, he could hold onto himself. He could feel the blood frenzy burning at his edges. If it had taken him over, he would have shoved all of himself inside and then done much worse.

"Not much," he said, his voice thick with heat and relief. "You are taking me so well."

"Back at you, big guy." Her eyes slammed shut on the next thrust, a high groan spilling out of her. There was no fear anymore, but Wick couldn't tell if that was because the lust was so big or because the amulet was still glowing.

Wick wanted to pound into her. Wanted to pull her into his lap and bounce her on his cock. Wanted to see how loud she got with all four ridges popping in and out of her, wanted to feel her flutter and spasm around him, he wanted to come inside her and eat it out of her. He was going to come, he could feel it pulsing in his cock.

He reached around her and touched her above her hole. There, just where the thick hair ended, was that tiny, swollen nub that had made her react so strongly when he'd licked it.

He rubbed it. Gently, like she'd told him to.

Briar yelled. Her hole contracted around him, squeezing him so tight she almost forced him out.

His hand slipped off her nub. He wrapped an arm around her waist, holding her still.

Briar moaned and shook, her open mouth pillowed on her arms. She let out another wordless cry as he found her nub again, so small and delicate he had to concentrate to keep touching it, his fingers threatening to slide off.

She moaned something. It took him several seconds to realize she was trying to speak.

"Circles," she panted in between thrusts. "Do... circles."

Dazed with his impending orgasm, Wick didn't

know what she meant. Then he understood, and he started rubbing circles against her small nub. It took all his concentration to keep his touch light, to keep his finger moving in circles against such a tiny target, but it was worth it to hear Briar come apart underneath him.

Briar let out a sob, her whole body taut. She smelled like salt and pleasure and sweet release, her inner walls growing even slicker as he pounded inside.

His third ridge slipped into her. Briar cried out again, reaching down to grab the arm he had secured across her waist.

Wick started, "I am going to—"

That was all he managed. He buried his nose in the back of her neck and came, three ridges deep, paralyzed as he rode out the waves of pleasure.

Finally, the waves subsided. He slumped, and Briar made a warning noise.

"Sorry," Wick attempted to say. It came out rough and nonsensical, and he pushed himself off of her with wobbly arms and fell onto his back beside her.

For a long minute, neither of them spoke.

Briar's chest heaved, glistening with sweat. "You're going to be a lot to get used to," she announced, then paused. "Not that we'll have much time to get used to each other. If we fly, this trip will barely take a week."

Wick nodded, strangely sad about it. A week was a blink for a Skullstalker.

"And then I will visit you in your riches," he confirmed.

Briar chuckled. Dirt stuck to her hair as she twisted

to look at him. "Sure, buddy. And I'll come and see you at your waterfall. Actually…"

Wick waited. "What?"

She shook her head. "Nothing. I'm going to let it be a surprise."

He frowned. But Briar didn't elaborate, only stretched mightily and winced.

Wick sat up, sniffing the air. No blood. The faintest scent of pain.

"How sore are you?" he asked.

"I told you, big boy. It's only the good kind of hurt." Briar closed one eye at him again.

"What does that mean?" Wick asked.

Briar hesitated. "Winking?"

He also meant "the good kind of hurt," which still did not make sense to him. But he nodded, assuming she was talking about the half-blink.

"It's, uh…" Briar grinned. "I wink when I'm trying to be charming, I guess. Is it not working?"

Wick thought about it. Briar was charming, but that was less important than all the other things. *Charming* felt like a mask she was putting on, like a smile she gave him to hide all the messy emotions clamoring under his nose.

"Yes," he said honestly. "But you do not need to be."

Briar's smile slipped. She stared at him with something very close to distrust. Then it opened into something he had seen several times over the last day: realization. She kept thinking he was lying to her. She did not yet know that he did not bother lying very often.

I don't trust easy, she had told him.

He believed her. Now he just needed to make her believe him: she did not need to be anything other than herself around him.

Briar averted her eyes, letting out a laugh that was much more stale than any laugh she'd produced today.

"Careful, big boy. Talk to strays like that and you might just talk them into staying." She stood, grimacing as she twisted to look at the dirt coating her backside. "Alright. Any chance you can sniff out the nearest river?"

SEVEN

Briar wanted to laugh as she scrubbed herself.

Wick had been so *eager* to find her a river. His tail had swished around like a pleased dog when she'd thanked him. She almost expected him to bark when he ran off to find her some more food.

Wick was stupidly sweet. She'd never had anyone so happy to do what she wanted. Even people she had blatantly manipulated. People she had tricked.

She didn't want to manipulate Wick. She actually wanted to *trust* him, which was ridiculous. She'd known the Skullstalker for a day and had let him fuck her on her hands and knees, a privilege she usually gave to people who she knew she could overpower.

She could never overpower Wick. And yet she had let him press her into the dirt, his arm locked around her middle, because what? She got *excited*?

Briar sighed and emptied a handful of river water over her face.

"You're only with him until you get to Marigold's," she reminded herself. "Do not let your guard down. And do *not* get attached."

Something moved in the corner of her eye. She stopped, her hands stilling in her damp hair.

If there was one thing she knew, it was when she was being watched.

She turned.

A water basilisk perched on the edge of the riverbank. Its beady eyes were fixed on her, its big, scaly body coiled in a way Briar really didn't like. She hadn't encountered many water basilisks, but she'd seen her fair share of regular ones, usually when she was trying to sneak through a dungeon.

This basilisk was ready to strike. And this wasn't some weak, underfed basilisk languishing in some nobleman's dungeons. This was a well-nourished bastard with gleaming scales and strong, sharp fangs and a strong snake body that was almost as big as her.

Briar eyed her pack. It was several feet away from the basilisk in the long grass, her dagger strapped to the side.

This is what I get for not staying close to my pack, Briar told herself. *Rookie mistake, Copperwood.*

Briar looked around, careful to only move her eyes. There were no rocks in reach to throw at it. What were the basilisk rules again? Make herself really big? No, it was moving slowly. Usually, she had a sword to stab them with, and she never had to worry about running into them in the wild.

"Nice basilisk," she whispered, bending as slowly as

she could manage. "Don't mind me. Just picking up a rock. Nothing to do with you."

The basilisk's eyes followed her as she moved. Briar stared back at it, cursing herself for being such a city dweller. She found herself in enough forests to know what to do with a damned water basilisk.

She dipped her hand in the water. The basilisk's tail twitched.

Briar tensed in preparation. Her hand closed carefully around a river rock. It was only as big as her fist. She would need to get in a good shot, then dive for her pack and hope for the best.

She drew her arm back to throw.

The basilisk lunged.

Briar swore and lobbed the river rock. It bounced off the basilisk's cheek, disrupting its path.

Briar dove for her pack. She could hear the basilisk hiss and rear up to follow, a flash of scales racing over the riverbank toward her. She braced herself to fight off a scaly body while she wrestled for the knife—

—only for a loud noise to make them both look up.

Wick sailed out of the sky, teeth bared.

He slammed into the basilisk feet-first. Scales and flesh splattered into the grass, the wet noise immediately drowned out by the agonized basilisk's scream.

Wick roared back at it. His wings flared, a clawed hand whipping out to slash the basilisk's throat in half.

The basilisk's cry fell silent. Its body fell into the grass, limp and partially headless.

Wick growled. His clawed foot rubbed against the

holes it had carved into the basilisk's body, as if he wanted to drag its head from its body entirely. Then he paused and turned to her. He had a sack over his shoulder, filled with fruit.

"Briar," he said. "Are you alright?"

Briar stared. She was propped up against the riverbank, naked and dripping. But she barely noticed the water running down her back or the grass against her hip. She was too busy gaping at Wick, who was standing over her with his claws bloody and his wings arched.

Several days ago, it would have been something out of her nightmares. Now, she was *touched*. Even as she tried to beat the feeling down, it made her heart flutter and her sore cunt throb.

Wick lifted his head. Sniffing the air, Briar realized. He was looking at her like he was searching for fang marks.

Briar pulled up a smile, wringing out her wet hair and flipping it over her shoulder in a way that drew focus to her bare, wet body. "My hero! You should become a guard. You would get a lot of coin."

"I am not made to be a guard," Wick said after a moment. His gaze had dropped to her breasts, she noted with pride. His attention was easier to deal with when he was interested in her body, not in her safety.

Briar climbed out of the river. "You're getting basilisk blood on my clothes."

"What? Oh." Wick stepped away from her pile of clothes. His claws had been dripping blood onto her pants, which were thankfully black for the very purpose of hiding blood.

He looked so concerned about her clothes that her heart clenched once more.

She stepped up to him. Despite all her intentions, her voice was annoyingly earnest as she said, "Really. Thank you for protecting me. I would have been basilisk food if you hadn't shown up."

Wick blinked. He held out the bag of fruit he had dangling from his non-bloody hand.

"I have fruit," he announced. "Like you wanted."

He held the bag open. Briar looked inside and saw a bundle of incredibly unripe apples, small, shiny, and green.

"Thank you," Briar said, still irritatingly touched. She forced her useless sentimentality back and made her smile sultry. "Fruit *and* protection. I need to thank you more thoroughly."

"You do not have to," Wick said.

Briar wanted to shake him. To demand that he act like a regular person, to drop all the sweet politeness and act more like the monster he was. Give her a proper reason to feel unsafe with him. If he kept being this good to her, there was nothing to do but get attached. And she didn't want to see how that ended.

But failing that, she would channel all her stupid, gooey feelings into something she could handle: good old-fashioned lust.

"No," she said softly. "I think I will."

With that, she sank to her knees in front of him.

Wick's tail swished uncertainly. "What are you doing?"

"Guess." She unknotted his loincloth, rubbing the material between her fingers. It was surprisingly clean for someone who slept in a nest.

The loincloth fell to the grass. Wick's cock was half-hard against his thigh, and Briar was a little smug at his fast reaction.

"But," Wick said, his tail swishing anxiously. "We've already—"

He cut off with a groan as she took his cock in his hand. She stroked it and watched it plump up under her touch. Her cunt tingled, still wet with his come.

Not now, she told it.

She stroked faster. His cock rose, but it didn't rise very far. It was too heavy to stand up against his stomach. The ridges were thick against her fingers, red and puffy.

Briar's mouth watered. She was still faintly appalled at herself for being attracted to a Skullstalker, a creature they used to scare children into behaving. But a nice cock was a nice cock, no matter what species it was attached to. And no matter how much it would make her jaw ache.

She tucked her wet hair behind her ears and leaned in, sliding her tongue through his slit.

Pre-come burst on her tongue, salty and bitter. She grinned and lapped it up.

Wick let out a low rumble. His hands clenched at his sides.

Briar huffed a laugh and pulled away. "You can touch my hair. Just don't push or pull me, or I'll bite."

She clicked her teeth together.

Wick nodded determinedly. Both his hands slid into her hair, his claws brushing her scalp. They were only half retracted, and Briar found she liked the light scrape.

She sucked the head into her mouth. Wick's hips jerked, his claws tightening in her hair.

Briar thought about pulling away and giving him another warning. But then he stilled, and Briar continued.

She liked knowing he was holding himself back. That he wanted her so badly he couldn't control himself, but he was forcing himself not to take it all.

The necklace glowed comfortingly between her damp breasts. Briar pulled back to give the tip of his cock a kiss and then sunk deeper, bobbing her head properly. She could barely fit her lips around him; forget about getting him into her throat. But he kept making small, shocked grunts like it was the best he'd ever had.

Briar let herself sink into the rhythm of it. But her jaw was already starting to ache, spit dripping down her chin from how wide she was stretched.

She pulled off reluctantly. Wick's hips jerked again, and his slick cockhead slid against her cheek.

"Eager," she said breathily.

"Sorry." Wick squeezed his eyes shut, but not in time to hide the pulsing fires in his eyes. He was shaking like she had taken him whole, not barely making it past the head.

She licked the first ridge, getting it shiny with spit. He still tasted faintly of her, and Briar heard herself groan.

Wick groaned with her. He was curling into himself, his wings pulled in tight to his back. The amulet glowed strongly between them, and Briar realized with some pride and some disappointment that he was going to come. She wanted to keep going, to taste him some more. Especially when he was being so *polite* about it.

His claws trembled against her scalp.

"I am going to come," he warned.

In response, she sucked his cock back into her mouth. It only took one more suck before he fulfilled his promise and came, hot ropes filling her mouth and spilling down her chin and chest.

She swallowed as best she could until his cock was spent and softening, Wick whimpering above her. Then she pulled off and wiped her chin, scooping more of it into her mouth. Mostly to watch the fire in his eyes flicker hotter, but partly to taste the evidence that she had done well.

Wick's wings and tail sagged, his shoulders heaving. "I was not inside you."

It took her a moment to understand what he meant. Briar laughed, stepping back into the river to clean her sticky chest.

"We're done for the day," she told him. "That was just a thank-you."

She wiped her chest clean and then got back onto the

riverbank, pulling her clothes back on. She was still damp, but she would dry.

"Sorry, I'm so small," she said as she laced her shirt up. "I suppose your other lovers were bigger. They would have to be, to fit that inside of them."

She motioned at his cock, which he was in the process of hiding behind his loincloth.

Wick finished tying his knot and paused. "I have never had a lover."

Briar laughed.

Wick didn't. He just stood there, watching her with the expression he'd been wearing for most of the blowjob: like he couldn't quite believe she was real.

Briar's laugh died. "Wait, are you serious? How old *are* you?"

"I have lost count," Wick said honestly. "Everyone I have attempted to mate with, I have killed and eaten."

Briar winced. She reached for her necklace, dragging it out to lie over her shirt laces.

"Right," she said. "I am glad we have this."

"As am I." Wick bowed his head. "I... I could feel the blood frenzy trying to take over. Every time."

He sounded so cautious. It annoyed Briar. Why couldn't he just hide his emotions like every other man? If he kept being all vulnerable like this, it would only make her like him more. The bastard.

Briar thought of his claws digging into her hips so hard he almost drew blood. Of those claws dragging against her scalp, his hips jerking, his breath coming fast, and the fire in his eyes swelling until they took over the black pools surrounding them.

And then he pulled back. Always, he came back to himself. Just like he'd always wanted. Briar winced as she imagined him coming out of a haze to find his hands covered in blood and viscera when all he'd wanted was a nice roll in his nest.

She forced her sorrow down. She couldn't afford to feel anything for Wick, no matter how sweet he was or how much his story affected her. They were two travelers stuck on a brief journey together, that was all.

"That must be why you're so intense," she said, trailing a hand down his arm. "Good thing I like it."

Wick watched her hand. "You do?"

Briar nodded. It scared her, obviously. But there was no lie in her voice as she admitted, "It's flattering. Knowing you want me so badly, you can't hold yourself back."

Wick frowned. "But I do hold back."

"Of course," she hurried to say. "Of course you do. The gentleman monster."

Wick's frown deepened. He cocked his head at her, like she was particularly puzzling, and he wanted to solve her.

Briar dropped her hand fast. She didn't want to be solved. She wanted to be safe and warm and full of life's other comforts, but she drew the line at being known.

Even Marigold, her oldest friend, didn't know her very well. Briar wasn't about to let a Skullstalker see her, *truly* see her, just because he kept saying things that soft-ened her tough heart.

She bent down to grab her pack. "Come on. We should get up in the air again."

Wick paused. He shifted his wings behind him, a pained expression flickering across his face.

Briar frowned. She had assumed he was lying about his wings hurting.

"Wick? Am I working you too hard?"

"I do not usually fly for this long," he admitted. "I will be fine."

He sniffed the air with a concerned expression.

Briar sighed. "What now?"

He pointed. Briar turned to see dark clouds massing on the horizon. The spring air was filled with the barest chill, barely noticeable under the warm breeze.

Briar snorted. "That storm is ages away. We can get some good flying time before it hits."

Eight

The storm wailed and crashed, icy water drilling against Wick's aching wings.

"Well," said Briar over the roaring rain. "At least, we have *some* shelter."

Wick nodded in agreement. His chin brushed the top of her head, an unavoidable circumstance of closing his wings around them both.

They had found a cave in the depths of the forest. But it was shallow, offering little shelter from the howling wind and rain. Wick had pulled her into his lap and closed his wings around her. Then he had ducked down into the haven he had made, shielding them from the elements.

Shielding *her*, anyhow. His face and most of his inner body were safe. But his back and his outer wings were still pelted with rain, cold and stinging as it rushed into the cave.

Briar peered up at him worriedly. Based on her squint, she could barely see him in the dim light.

"You really don't have to do this," she said.

"Mortals are fragile," he replied. "It takes more than a storm to harm a Skullstalker."

Briar rolled her eyes. "*Fragile*. You know how many storms I've been in?"

"You are shivering," he pointed out.

Briar tensed, as if she could beat her body's reactions with sheer stubbornness. The cold won, another shiver running through her small frame.

He rubbed her arms cautiously, as he had seen her do when the cold wind started. According to Briar, they were maybe three days of flying away from her witch's cottage.

I'm guessing, she had said through chattering teeth. *Never flown before you. Don't quite know how much time it takes to get anywhere on wings.*

Briar eyed his hands on her arms so closely he wondered if he had forgotten to retract his claws.

Then she smiled, small and warped, like she was trying to hold it back.

"Thanks, sweet thing," she said. "But you're almost as cold as the rain."

Wick let go of her arms and leaned back as much as he could. But she was in his lap, and there was only so far he could go before he started breaking the sealed cocoon of his wings, and he didn't want to let any rain in.

"How quickly do mortals die from cold?" he asked.

"I'm not going to wither away in your arms, Wick." Briar paused, tilting her head consideringly. "Actually, let me try something."

She knelt up in his lap and looked deep into his eyes.

Wick's wings spasmed. His whole body had been doing that more since Briar arrived—tail twitching, wings flinching, body reacting for reasons he could not control. His brother Slate liked to tease him for his body giving away his emotions. Apparently, Wick was having more emotions than ever because he constantly found himself moving in ways he didn't even notice until it was over.

Briar leaned up even further. Her eyes were just as stunningly blue as the first night they met. The kind of blue that made him want to dive in.

Briar's lips parted. She tucked in so close he could feel her chest move with her breath. He waited for her to smile, as she often did when she caught his eye. But she just knelt in his lap, watching him with an unknowable expression.

Wick wondered if she would kiss him. He had seen mortals kiss. It seemed nice. But looking down at her right now, he felt it would be significantly better than *nice*. He craved it like he craved blood during a frenzy. If she looked at him any longer, he was going to—

Briar ducked her head, and the smile bloomed, so bright it knocked the breath from his lungs.

"Your eyes are warm," she explained, looking back up at him.

Wick blinked. Then he remembered the fire in his eyes, a rarity in Skullstalkers that he often forgot about. He did not have a mirror, after all. And his fiery eyes performed no useful function.

Until now, at least.

"You should stay close," Wick suggested.

"Good idea," Briar whispered back. She bit her lip. Her gaze fell from him again, and Wick wondered if she feared being so close to him, despite all her time clutched to his chest during their flight.

He sniffed the air. Rain and cold and sweat, but no fear. He couldn't think of anything else that would make her keep looking away like that.

He tucked away the urge to kiss her. Maybe next time they mated, he would ask for it.

"You must be tired," Briar said finally. "All this flying."

"It is nothing." Wick rolled his shoulders. They *were* profoundly sore. He had almost been glad to feel that first raindrop that meant they needed to stop and find shelter.

"Still," Briar said. "I should give you a massage when this storm clears up."

"Massage," Wick repeated.

"It's where I knead your muscles and make them less sore." Briar held up her hands to form makeshift claws. It was awkward; there was not much room to move around in the safety of his sore wings.

"I'll show you tomorrow," she said.

Wick nodded. He looked forward to it. He looked forward to anything that involved her touching him.

Rain battered his wings. A particularly strong gust of wind lashed the cave, and Wick braced himself around Briar.

Briar watched his wing muscles flex with effort.

"My hero," she said, voice unusually high. She cleared her throat and pulled her smile back into place. "So! Since we're stuck here until the storm passes, pressed uncomfortably close and now apparently staring at each other for warmth, we should play a game."

"A game," Wick repeated. It sounded suspiciously like a mating proposition, which would be difficult with them hiding inside his wings.

"Yes," Briar said eagerly. "A question game. Each of us asks each other a question, one after another."

Wick thought about it. "Where do your scars come from?"

Briar's eyes widened. "Well! Starting out strong."

Wick waited. Briar cleared her throat, shifting her damp hair out of her eyes. He wanted to follow it with his claw, tuck it behind her ear like she was doing. There was a daintiness to her actions, just as much as there was a roughness. She balanced between the two with a captivating quality.

"Nowhere in particular," she said. "Just the usual sort of tokens from the life I live."

It was a pale answer. Wick touched her ribs through her laced shirt, feeling them contract under his touch. He had only seen her naked a handful of times, but he could remember every inch of her. There was a slash scar over her torso.

"Here?" he asked.

Briar's eyelashes fluttered. Her mouth moved wordlessly, and Wick was helpless to do anything but stare at it. Even with her scars, she was the softest thing he had ever touched.

"A knife fight," she said breathlessly. "A few years back. I wasn't even involved; I was just unlucky enough to be standing there."

Wick's hand migrated to her back, touching a burn scar through the wet fabric. "And this?"

Briar's throat worked. She swayed back, and for a moment, Wick feared he had pressed too far. Was it her turn to ask? She hadn't clarified how the question game worked.

"I—I was paid to smuggle something from a kitchen," she said, too fast. "A ledger. The cook caught me, pushed me up against a boiling cauldron. My shirt burned onto my back."

It was not a particularly brutal explanation. But the image would have made Wick grimace if he truly believed it.

"You're lying," he said.

Briar blinked rapidly. A shocked grin spread over her face. "Excuse me?"

"Why do you lie?" Wick asked. "I will not tell anyone."

Briar laughed. One of her nervous ones—still charming, still sweet. But nervous. He was beginning to tell the difference.

"I'm..." Briar paused, looking up at him with that wary look that she rarely let slip through. "I'm not worried about you telling. I just don't tell people these things."

"Why?"

"Do you go around spilling your life story to anyone who asks?"

"Nobody has asked," Wick said honestly.

Briar said nothing. Her chest rose and fell against his own. A small shiver ran through her, and Wick itched to rub her arms again. If only his touch would help as much as his fiery eyes.

"It's not a terribly interesting story," she said finally. "I was trying to save a dog."

"A dog?"

Briar sighed, annoyed. "I was young. Hadn't learned that you save yourself and you don't look back. I woke up to an inn burning down around me, so I leapt out a window. I was about to run into the streets, find some-where else to hide—the city guard was on my tail that month—but I heard a dog barking."

Her mouth twitched. She still looked annoyed, but now it was a mask she was using to hide whatever was happening underneath.

Wick sniffed the air. Rain, cold... and sadness. Not much. Just enough to smell it under the storm, soft and heavy.

"There was a retired hunting dog," she continued.

"He lived at the inn. Old, deaf thing. Could barely walk, but the owners kept it around anyway."

"You went back in to save it," Wick prompted.

Briar laughed bitterly. "I did! Got that scar for my troubles."

Thunder crashed outside the cave. Wick tightened his wings, pressing harder into Briar's back, right against the healed burn.

Briar's lack of speech was enough. But Wick asked anyway.

"Did you save it?"

"No," Briar replied after a moment. "It was a good lesson. Save yourself, don't look back."

The sadness swelled between them, thick in Wick's nostrils. It was edged with a dozen other emotions Wick couldn't identify, everything mixing into an incomprehensible blur. But none of them were particularly pleasant.

Then Briar blinked, and her smile was back.

"Anywho," she said, smiling despite all the emotions curling through the cramped space between them. "After that depressing answer, it's my turn. You mentioned your brother, Slate. You said he had a wife? I've never heard of a lady Skull-stalker."

"There are some," Wick said. "But she is not a Skull-stalker. Ruby was a mortal."

Briar's blond brows rose. "*Was?*"

"When they were first courting, yes. Now she is... more."

"More," Briar repeated. "Wait, a Skullstalker courted a *mortal*? That's ridiculous."

Wick fought back a confusing tangle of hurt. He had thought the same thing when Slate had explained the situation. But they were very good together.

"What is she now?" Briar continued.

"A god," Wick replied. "Or half a god. Mortals die too quickly. Slate would have been bereft if she had died in a mere two hundred years."

"Two hundred—?" Briar cut off, shaking her head. "Al*right*. Did he do that to her? Make her a god?"

"Half-god," he reminded her. "And no, she did it to herself. Later, Slate found a way to tie their lifespans together so she would not die before him."

"How?"

Wick's tail flicked underneath him, remembering that strange, misty cave he had walked into with Slate at his side. The scarred Skullstalker that had awaited them, his bone mask chipped with age.

"We met a sorcerer, of a sort. He lives in a far-off land. I have only met him once. He is the one who told me my blood frenzy cannot be cured."

"Well," Briar said quietly. "I hope he's wrong."

"I hope so too. But I doubt it. He is a Skullstalker. Your witch is just a mortal. She *is* mortal, yes?"

"Marigold? As mortal as they come."

Another crash of thunder echoed through the cave. Rain pelted Wick's wings, leaving him glad that Skullstalkers were less sensitive to the elements.

Briar shivered.

Wick drew her closer. "Tell me about her."

Briar looked up at him, his fire reflecting in her eyes. "Follow the game rules, Wick. It has to be a question."

"What is she like?"

Briar smiled, small and real. "Marigold is... my friend. My only true friend, I guess. We met as children, back when we were still at the orphanage. Then we struck out on our own. Petty thievery, mostly. She got caught pickpocketing a powerful sorcerer. When he saw her magical abilities, he took her under his wing. Of course, I got tossed to the side of the road. No magical ability in me."

"I am sorry," Wick said.

Briar shrugged. "It turned out alright. She kept in touch, which was more than I expected. We even help each other out sometimes. What about you? How was the mighty Skullstalker's childhood?"

"I barely remember," Wick admitted. "I slept. I ate. I explored."

"Alone?"

Wick nodded. Older Skullstalkers, like Slate, had memories of growing up together in a cave. Wick had no memories of togetherness. He hadn't even known he was a Skullstalker until he encountered one during a hunt. He had examined the Skullstalker's corpse after the blood frenzy ended and found the body to be closer to his own than any other creature he had met.

Slate had found him not long after. Wick had wandered into his realm entirely by accident, and Slate had guided him out, suspicious all the while.

I am used to my younger siblings lunging for my throat the first chance they get, he had said.

I will try not to lunge, Wick had replied. It had amused Slate enough that he explained more about their species.

"We live isolated lives," Wick said, then hesitated. "I did try to make friends."

Briar winced. "How did that go?"

"How you would imagine." Wick fell silent, remembering so many creatures fleeing from him. Watching them vanish into the distance became preferable to the alternative.

"I think I told them to hurt me," Wick continued. "But so far, no one has managed it."

Briar looked at his body, which was covered in various scars. There were even some in his skull mask, the most prominent one chipping away the bone above his mouth.

"I am glad you have that necklace," he said.

It was not the first time he had told her, but it had a different effect. Briar looked at him like he had said something very serious. His fiery eyes reflected in hers, and the air hung heavily with anticipation.

Then Briar looked away, laughing breathlessly. "Well, *I* am glad we fucked before the storm caught us. It would be pretty impossible to do the deed in time like this."

Wind howled around the cave. Wick tightened his wings around Briar until he could feel every lift and fall of her breath, her face so close to his that her nose brushed his chin.

He would like it, he realized. Mating like this. Holding her close as she rocked against his lap. His wings tucking her close and shutting out the rest of the world.

Briar shivered.

Wick leaned in closer, trying to force the fire in his eyes to swell. "Are you still cold?"

Briar swallowed. Despite the warmth they offered, she seemed to have a difficult time meeting his eyes.

"I'm getting warmer," she said softly.

NINE

Briar woke up to the sound of a small explosion.

She lifted her groggy head from her pack.

Wick was sitting in the mouth of the cave they had sheltered in. The sun streamed in behind him, illuminating the damp rocks and a badly constructed campfire.

Wick held up a stick. There was a shattered egg tied to it, patches of shell and yolk dripping down into the fire and baking onto the burning wood.

"It did not cook as it should," Wick said crossly.

Briar giggled. She sat up, surprised to find that most of her clothes had dried overnight. Her underclothes were still slightly damp, but otherwise she was warm and dry. Thanks to Wick's protection, of course.

"You need to heat up a stone," she explained. "And then crack the eggs onto the stone. Or, even more ideal, find a frypan."

"Oh." Wick stared down at the exploded egg. The

string he'd tied around it was starting to burn, along with the stick. "That is not self-evident."

"My fault," Briar said, unable to hold back a grin. "I should have explained. Good thing we still have your fruit!"

She heaved her pack into her lap and pulled out the bag of awful, underripe apples he had picked for her yesterday. After growing up at an orphanage and on the streets, there wasn't much that could turn her stomach.

Wick stood. He had to stoop, his horns and wingtips scraping the top of the cave. He stamped out the fire and turned to her.

"You will need more than that," he said, nodding at the apple she was munching on.

Briar forced down a surge of warmth that had risen, unwelcome, in her traitorous chest. He still didn't know much about mortals, but he was paying attention. Now he knew basic things, like that she needed more than fruit to tide her over.

She swallowed her underripe fruit. "How are your wings?"

Wick held them out gingerly, considering. His hesitation was enough.

Briar patted the ground in front of her. It was still damp, but barely.

"Come on," she said. "I owe you a massage."

Wick's wings pulled in protectively. "You will... 'knead' my muscles?"

"It doesn't hurt! I promise." Briar flashed him a smile. He didn't seem soothed, which was annoyingly typical of him. Briar had a fantastic track record of making men believe her just by shoving her attractiveness in their faces. But apparently, it didn't work so well on Skullstalkers.

"It doesn't hurt *much*," she amended through a mouthful of apple. She patted the ground again. "Come on! What harm can one itty bitty mortal do?"

This seemed to mollify him. He sat down in front of her, only turning around when she instructed.

Briar finished her apple and threw the core over her shoulder, considering his back. It was huge and solid, rippling with muscles and scars. His wings narrowed at the base before blending effortlessly with his pale skin.

Briar tried to look confident. Wick couldn't see her, but holding herself confidently was almost as good as actually feeling confident. She was a good liar, even to herself.

"Spread your wings," she said.

With a grunt, Wick did. The grunt was the only sign that he was in more pain than he'd let on. She had caught him wincing several times as they soared down to this cave, but he had denied it when she'd called him on it.

His wings scraped both sides of the cave. Briar didn't pay them much mind. She only told him that because stretching had to be good after being stuck in a cramped cave all night. Skullstalker or mortal, muscles were muscles.

Briar started on his shoulders. She had to kneel up to reach the top of them, squeezing hard. Most of her massages were to seduce someone. But this was a real massage, and that called for force.

Wick grunted louder. "So, when you said *knead*—"

"I meant it." Briar squeezed harder, feeling the muscles resist underneath her touch. They were tight, just like she thought. She moved down lower, feeling the pale skin around the base of his wings. The muscles were knotted, and Briar winced in sympathy.

Wick's wings twitched.

"Stay," she warned him.

Wick sat up straight, sitting so still she couldn't see him breathe. Briar kneaded his back harder, basking in having a man listen to her so thoroughly. Especially a man like Wick, with his immense power. His *size*. She had met many big, powerful men, but she hadn't wanted any of them like Wick. She'd never trusted them enough. But Wick...

Wick was ridiculously sweet. Shockingly gentle. And all too eager to please. A dangerous combination that made Briar want him to hold her down and do absolutely anything to her. Because, for once, she almost had faith that he would only do what she wished.

Wick made a surprised noise, pulling her out of her thoughts.

"Does it hurt?" she asked.

"No," Wick said slowly. "Not... entirely. It is a strange sensation."

Briar snickered. "Isn't it? My first massage, I almost kicked Marigold in the face. Am I getting deep enough?"

She pushed her thumbs into his joints as hard as she could.

Wick flinched. Then he stopped, holding himself so still that Briar wanted to praise him. She held back on it, kneading harder into the stubborn knot of muscles.

Slowly, Wick's rigid posture relaxed. "Oh."

"That sounded like a good noise," Briar said.

"It was," Wick said thoughtfully. "I feel... looser."

"That's the idea." Briar smiled to herself, moving over to the next knot around his wings.

Wick rumbled. His skin was warming slowly under her touch.

It took several minutes for Briar to realize he was leaning back into her, pressing back against her hands.

"Hey," she said gently. "Sit up properly."

Wick made a sleepy noise and straightened.

First massage, Briar reminded herself. It got her thinking about the *other* first times she'd given him—a fact that she still couldn't believe. Before her, he had never put that gorgeous cock in anything. It was a waste. And it made it more surprising that he kept holding himself back when he was fucking her. Anyone else would have taken advantage.

She wondered if he had kissed anyone. If he'd gotten that far with any of those unfortunate creatures he'd attempted to fuck before the blood frenzy took over. She hoped so. It would be sad if he got given sex before a kiss.

Briar had come close to kissing him last night. Just for a moment, just when she had been gazing into his fiery eyes and feeling their warmth on her cheeks. She didn't know how she could feel such fondness for black orbs filled with flames, but somehow Wick made it easy.

Wick slumped, his shoulders drooping.

"Feels good?" Briar asked gently.

Wick rumbled. His tail curled absentmindedly against Briar's arm.

Affection surged through Briar's chest as she watched his tail grip loosely around her wrist. Whether he meant to do this or not, it was deeply cute. It made her think of how closely he held her at night, of how much he was leaning into her touch right now. He obviously enjoyed the closeness. And he'd so obviously been starved for it.

A dozen impossible futures raced through Briar's mind. She shoved them down and pushed harder against Wick's lax back.

He'll have all the chances in the world to find someone to cuddle with after he cures his blood frenzy, she reminded herself. *Once they stop screaming, anyway.*

Her kneading slowed until she was sitting there with her hands flat against his back. He was breathing slowly, peacefully. An ancient monster, utterly sweet and lovely under her touch.

She smoothed her hands over his back one last time. Then she leaned back, pulling up a smile.

"I think that will do the job," she said with more softness than she would usually allow.

Wick hummed. But he didn't move.

Briar leaned around him. Wick's fiery eyes were closed, his head drooping toward his chest.

"Hey." Briar pushed him gently. "Wakey-wakey, Mr. Skullstalker."

Wick grunted. He listed sideways, leaning against the wall of the cave. Falling asleep, Briar realized.

Briar touched the tail that was curled around her wrist and thought about curling up beside him. Feeling those big arms close around her like she'd felt for several nights now. Letting him get closer than most men she slept with, especially any man since she'd been cursed.

But it was a slippery slope. Briar knew herself enough to know that she couldn't let herself get too close. The longer this journey went on, the more danger she was in.

Briar pulled his tail from her arm and gave it a soft tug.

Wick's head jerked up. He twisted to look back at her, blinking sleepily.

"Come on, big boy," Briar said. "We need to get moving."

Briar was right, the massage *did* help.

But only so much. Wick could fly a few hours at a time. Which still made for fast travel, but it cut Briar's estimated travel time by several days.

"We're reaching the edge of the forest," Briar told him as they prepared for another night in a mossy clearing. "Mountains are coming up."

"I can smell them in the air," Wick said.

His voice was strange. Briar paused in the middle of stamping out their campfire and looked over.

Wick was standing in the middle of the clearing, staring up at the trees. His head was raised, like he really was smelling them.

Briar asked, "What do they smell like?"

Wick said nothing. His head raised further. A cool breeze rolled around the clearing, making Briar shiver.

"Snow, I would imagine," she said, louder.

Wick startled. He looked back at her, blinking as if she had awoken him from a dream. "What? Yes. That's... mostly right."

Briar narrowed her eyes at him. "Why are you acting strange?"

"I am not." Wick frowned. He looked up again, even though the mountains weren't visible from here. "I just haven't smelled them in a long time."

"Oh?" Briar dropped to her knees in the moss, wincing as the movement made her cunt throb—and not in a good way. Wick's length was heavenly, but too many days of use had made it difficult to sit down.

"Why not?" Briar continued.

Wick was silent. His wings flexed distractedly as he stared in the direction of the mountains.

"I was born there," he said. "I have not been back since I was small."

Briar thought about saying something humorous, like not being able to imagine him small. But Wick looked so lost in thought. She patted the moss next to her instead.

"Well, let me take your mind off it," she said, her voice dropping low and sultry.

That jolted Wick out of his thoughtful stupor. His head snapped toward her so fast that Briar giggled.

"Eager," she commented. She sat up on her knees, grateful for the soft moss after many nights on the hard dirt. "Come on, big boy. Light my fire."

He looked at her with that confused look that meant she had said another mortal phrase he didn't understand, but he dropped obediently to his knees in front of her. Briar took a moment to bask in it; even on his knees, he still towered over her. His arms were as thick as her whole body, his claws as long as her fingers. And yet he waited for her assent to touch her.

Briar grinned. "So. We're going to do something different tonight."

"Different," Wick repeated.

His cock was already getting hard under his loincloth. Briar eyed it joyously and then focused back on his face.

"You might have noticed you are *significantly* larger than me," she began. "And you know how much I enjoy that."

"You have smelled less of fear the past few nights," he agreed.

Briar held her smile in place. She didn't want to be reminded that he could smell her emotions, and she definitely didn't want to think about why she wasn't scared of him anymore. She should be scared. Scared was a *sensible* emotion when she was dealing with a literal monster. And yet, she couldn't help but trust the bony bastard.

"Nevertheless," she said. "I don't think I can take your cock tonight."

Wick's tail flicked in concern. "But your curse—"

Said curse flared quietly in Briar's gut. Not painful, not yet. But warm enough to make itself known, creeping forever toward her heart.

"Not in *that* hole," Briar continued, cutting him off. "But thankfully, I have several. And thankfully, the curse counts ass fucking as sex."

Wick's tail stilled. For a moment, he said nothing, staring down at her while his fiery eyes swelled with light.

"Oh," he said finally, his eyes smoking with heat. "Good."

Briar was feeling *especially* grateful for the moss as she trembled against it some time later, her knees quaking with the effort of holding her up.

Her arms had given out several minutes ago. She crouched with her cheek pillowed on her arms, groaning with each pass of Wick's giant fingers.

"How does it feel?" she panted. "Huh? Do I feel good on your fingers?"

Wick nodded. He was bent over her, kissing her shoulders in a way that made her want to turn around and grab him, start kissing him properly. But he seemed to be greatly enjoying the revelation that he could kiss her body while he stretched her, and she couldn't muster the effort to turn around right now.

"Feels different," Wick said against her skin. "It

doesn't end like your other hole. Do you think I can fit all of me inside?"

Briar groaned and reached underneath herself to toy with her clit. "*Gods*. Let's find out."

Wick hesitated. "But you said this hole isn't wet enough."

"Not yet." Briar looked back at him, her cheeks burning with anticipation. "You can get hard again, can't you?"

Wick nodded, confused.

Briar wiggled her ass, feeling her hole clench around his fingers. "Then get me wet, big boy."

Wick blinked. Then he jerked back, pulling his fingers out of her so fast that Briar gasped. Her eyes fell to his hard cock, which was bright red and jumped under his touch.

"That's it," Briar coaxed as Wick gripped himself. "Come on me. Stuff it in my hole."

Wick groaned. His head tipped back, his chest heaving as his hand blurred over his cock. Briar watched it, panting against her arms. It conjured a hundred images of Wick doing this to himself alone in his cave, or his mountain, or wherever else he had lived over the centuries. Millennia? Briar had always heard Skullstalkers lived for thousands of years, but he said he was younger.

Wick let out a low growl. A full-body shudder worked through him, his wings snapping out as he came, thick ropes of come splashing over Briar's bare back.

Briar grinned. She waited for Wick's fiery eyes to pry open again, then wiggled her ass.

"Messy," she goaded. "Clean me up."

Wick made an unintelligible noise and started running a finger through the come on her back, feeding it into her stretched hole.

Briar's eyelids fluttered. She had mostly agreed with his "fitting" question to make him hot, but now she was genuinely giddy about the idea. *Could* he fit inside her like this?

Wick scooped another fingerful of come inside her. His eyes were half-lidded, his mouth hanging open as he watched it squeeze inside her.

"Remember to slick yourself up," Briar reminded him.

Wick did, a growl cutting off in his throat. He gripped her hip and met her eyes questioningly.

Briar braced her knees against the moss. "Give me all you got, big boy."

Wick's hand trembled on her hip as he guided himself in.

Briar bit her arm in ecstasy as he started to thrust. Gently, as he always did at first. Working himself in. He'd stretched her for so long there wasn't even a sting, just a powerful stretch as he pushed inside.

Briar cried out as the first ridge popped inside... then the second.

"Ohhhh *gods*," she groaned, her eyes falling shut. She curled her hands against the moss, ripping out soft tufts. Anal wasn't often her preference, but the sensation of those ridges made it entirely worth it.

Wick leaned back to watch his cock vanish into her

hole. A harsh growl ripped out of him, trailing off into a moan.

"You're stretched so *wide*," he panted admiringly.

He pushed deeper. The third ridge popped inside, so fast that Briar yelled in shock. She tried to say something, but Wick was shoving inside with a roughness that could only mean one thing.

Briar pried her eyes open just as the amulet started to glow against the moss, lighting up the dark clearing.

Wick's animal grunting grew quieter. His thrusts gentled, his hands trembling on her hips from holding himself back.

Good boy, Briar thought. But before she could say it, Wick's arms were closing around her thighs and hauling her into his lap.

Briar's yelp turned into a moan as he pulled her deeper onto his cock. Then he lifted her again, pulling her up and down on his cock.

Like a toy, Briar thought, dazed. Her mouth hung open in shocked pleasure, noises jolting out of her that she'd never heard herself make. She clung to his arms, her head falling back against his chest as he lifted her, dragging her back down and spearing her deeper and deeper.

We might really do it, she thought, feeling the tip of that fourth and final ridge bump against her entrance.

"So *full,*" Wick slurred. "So full of me. *Look.*"

He hooked his chin over her head, staring down. Briar followed his gaze and cried out at the sight; every time he thrust inside, a bulge appeared in her stomach.

Briar gaped. She felt so *full*. And now she finally looked at it, her belly stretching with each thrust.

Wick growled desperately. His hot breath clouded over her hair, coming in hot gusts with every thrust. His thrusts stuttered, his noises getting louder.

The final ridge met her entrance again. Briar wriggled uselessly in his grip, straining to get it inside her on the downstroke.

"Please," she heard herself say. "Gods, *please* give it to me. Give me all of it."

Wick roared. The noise echoed around the clearing, making birds take off from trees. Briar barely noticed. He was so impossibly huge inside her, her clit throbbing with every thrust.

"Yes," Briar groaned as Wick bounced her deeper. "Yes, just like—"

Wick's huge hand slapped over her mouth. He stilled with it, leaving Briar to whine and struggle against his iron hold.

Wick shushed her. It took Briar an embarrassingly long moment to realize his head was cocked. Listening.

She stilled along with him, trembling with effort. He was still inside her, that fourth ridge seated right against her entrance.

At first, there was nothing. Then the low murmur of voices. A man's voice echoed near the clearing:

"What in the void was that?"

TEN

Wick's first reaction was deep, unstoppable dread.

I am going to kill them, he thought, horror creeping in around the blinding lust. *They will attack, and I will kill them all, and then Briar—*

The thought came to an abrupt halt as his arm brushed the necklace around Briar's neck. It had activated during their mating, as it always did. Keeping the blood frenzy away.

The relief was short-lived. The mortals were coming closer.

"Shit," Briar whispered.

Wick grunted in agreement and stood. Briar's breath hitched, her hands tightening around his arms as he shifted inside her.

Wick carried her behind a wide tree trunk and pressed her against it, hiding her from the clearing. If they were quiet enough, surely the mortals would walk by without incident.

There were three men. He could smell them, stinking of dirt and sweat and fresh pig meat. They were coming back from a hunt.

"Over here," the first one called, old and croaky.

Briar's cheek twisted against the bark to look at him.

"Keep going," she whispered. "Just be quiet."

Her hole spasmed around him, and Wick held back a groan.

A small part of Wick warned him that this was a bad idea. The men were almost on them. But Briar's hips were working, trying to get him deeper. He'd almost fit his last ridge inside her. They were so *close*.

"Come on," Briar whispered pleadingly. "I need it."

Wick held back a growl and resumed his thrusts. He kept them soft and shallow, not daring to jolt her against the rough bark. He didn't even try to push his last ridge inside her, even though he could hear her biting back a whimper every time it brushed her entrance.

The three men emerged into the clearing. Two of them were holding crossbows, the third was clutching a dagger nervously, a dead pig hanging over his shoulder.

"Fire's not long gone," said the first man, kicking at the ash heap that was once their campfire. "Camp's still set up. Can't see any struggle."

"I didn't hear shit," said the man in the middle. He turned to the pig man. "Sure you heard something, Pen?"

"I *swear* it was this way," said Pen, shoving the pig's

snout out of the way of his dagger. "You heard it, right, Vern?"

Vern grunted. He was in front, an old scar closing one eye permanently. The other eye roved the clearing, not faltering on where Wick was mating Briar quietly behind a tree.

"Heard somethin'," said Vern quietly. "'Cept if it's what I *think* I heard, we'd already be dead."

If Wick weren't so focused on mating quietly, he would have been annoyed. He wished his siblings in the mortal realm weren't so bloodthirsty. They gave Skull-stalkers a bad name.

Briar let out a tiny gasp.

Wick covered her mouth again. Briar's eyelids fluttered, her hole squeezing around him so tightly that Wick let out his own noise, rough and guttural.

The men in the clearing froze. Vern clicked something in his crossbow, eyes scanning the clearing warily.

"Earnest," he said to the second man. "You hear it now?"

"Sure do, boss," Earnest whispered, clutching his crossbow tightly. "Sure it sounds Skull-like?"

"I know animals," Vern said. "That ain't animal. That's a monster."

Wick gritted his fangs and thrust faster. For some reason, the idea that they would get caught made him harder. His cock swelled inside Briar, a telltale sign that he was about to come.

Briar panted under his hand. Lust rolled off her in waves, so hot and tantalizing that Wick's mouth watered.

He squeezed his eyes shut, thrusting as fast as he dared.

"Can't tell where it came from," came Pen's nervous voice as Wick's hips started to stutter. "What do we do, Vern?"

Vern said something. Wick didn't hear it. His orgasm flooded through his body as powerfully as any frenzy, and he pinned Briar into the bark as he filled her. Waves of pleasure unlike any he'd ever known before Briar rolled through him, so intense his legs threatened to give out.

Wick dug his claws into the tree and bit down hard on his tongue. It didn't help. A growl ripped out of his throat, low and unmistakable. Briar whined underneath it, the sound so delicious that Wick pulsed once more, feeling it drip out of her hole and down his balls.

The clearing went silent.

Wick held his breath. Briar's hot breath dragged against his palm, her bright eyes pinned on him as they waited.

Vern burst through the trees, his crossbow raised. His hard expression dropped into disgust as he took in the sight in front of him.

"Void take me," he snarled. "Unhand her, monster!"

"Okay, let's wait *one* moment—" Briar's breathy reply cut off with a yelp as the crossbow let fly.

Wick grabbed it out of the air and crushed it in his hand. It would have hit his chest, he realized. That was good. As long as they didn't hurt Briar.

He slipped out of her, ignoring her gasp as he placed her back on the ground.

"If everyone could *wait*," Briar said, louder.

But horrified gasps were coming up behind them. Wick turned to see Earnest, his face twisted in shock and his crossbow raised. Pen stood behind him, gaping, his arms going so slack the pig dropped out of them.

The dead pig hit the floor. Earnest fumbled with his crossbow, another arrow letting fly.

Wick caught it and roared. The amulet was glowing again, smudged with sweat where it hung between Briar's breasts. It was the only thing keeping Wick from tearing into all these men without mercy. He could feel the blood frenzy bubbling up inside his skull like a wildfire.

"You horrid *beast*," Vern spat, reloading his crossbow. "Fear not, maiden! We will save you!"

"Oh, come *on*," Briar complained.

Wick leapt back into the clearing. There were too many weapons, and he didn't want one of them to get careless and strike Briar by accident. His loincloth was in a pile next to the ashy campfire, but he ignored it as he turned to face the three men, two of whom were running at him with crossbows and one of whom was standing back and looking like he might be sick.

"Flank him," Vern barked. "Get 'im, Earn!"

"I got him, I got him," Earnest croaked, his hands shaking as he pointed his reloaded crossbow at Wick's head.

Arrows flew. Wick caught one. The other one flashed past his arm, dragging a divot of flesh out with it.

Wick snarled reflexively. "Stop! I mean you no harm!"

Behind them, Pen made a noise of confusion that reminded Wick very much of how Briar had reacted when he had spoken to her for the first time. Obviously, the stories they heard of Skullstalkers did not include much talking, much less asking for peace.

"Get 'im," Vern yelled again, sweat beading on his forehead as he reloaded.

Wick prepared for another onslaught.

Briar ran out of the trees, waving her arms.

"OI," she yelled. "CUT THAT OUT!"

Everybody stopped. Briar walked in front of Wick and stood, naked and glistening, her arms raised defensively.

Vern was the first to recover. He raised his crossbow, pointing it at Wick's head. "Young maiden, move."

"*You* move," Briar replied. "You're ruining my night."

The men traded a confused look. The pig that Pen had been trying to pick up slipped through his grip yet again, slapping to the mossy ground.

"But," Earnest tried. "But he was ravishing you."

"He was!" Briar smiled brightly. "And if you don't mind, I'd like for him to get back to it. So if you wouldn't mind getting out of my sight, I'd appreciate it."

With that, she bent down to snag her shirt from the ground.

"But," Earnest said again. He turned to Vern, looking lost.

"What sort of unnatural woman are you?" Verne asked, horrified. "You bedded a *Skullstalker*?"

"Well, no mortal could satisfy me." Briar gave him

another sunny smile as she wriggled into her pants. "You can leave now. Feel free to leave the pig, I'm getting hungry."

Pen looked expectantly at Vern, his arms loosening like he was actually thinking about leaving the pig. Then he noticed Vern's disgusted expression and grabbed it tightly again.

Vern's nostrils flared. "Void take you," he snapped. "If you don't know what's good for ya, we'll sort you out. You're comin' with us."

He took a step toward Briar.

Wick growled. He stepped in front of Briar, his wings flaring out warningly.

"Just try it," he snarled.

Briar's grin turned threatening as she watched Vern. Wick had never seen a smile do that before. It was intriguing.

"And how are you going to take me?" she asked, her calm hiding bloodshed behind it. "Three mortals against a Skullstalker and his pissed off woman. You might as well place your heads in his mouth."

Pen cleared his throat. "I-I think we should get out of here, boss. Right, Earn?"

Earnest said nothing. He was looking at Briar with the same confusion as before, scratching his head like he was still trying to make sense of what he was seeing.

Vern spat on the mossy ground. "You shit on everything natural and good. I hope you're happy with your—your husband of nightmares!"

In terms of insults, it was nothing Wick was not used

to. But Briar let out a snarl of her own, her hand flexing on her undone belt like she was going to pull out her dagger.

"Oh yeah?" she called after Vern as he stormed off, the other two men trailing behind him. "Well, fuck you! He's better than any mortal I've ever met!"

Wick blinked. Nobody had ever said anything so kind about him.

Briar sighed, turning back to him and running a hand through her sweaty hair, picking out bark. "That was *not* a good comeback. Why didn't you stop me?"

Wick did not respond. A strange feeling was swelling within him, a quiet pleasure that had last occurred when he was watching a waterfall several decades ago.

Briar's hand slowed in her hair, pinching a shred of bark. "What?"

"Do you mean that?" Wick asked. "That I am..."

He trailed off. Saying it suddenly felt too vulnerable.

Briar dropped her gaze. She flicked the bark from her hair and laughed, nervousness wafting off her in waves.

"Sure," she said lightly. "You're, you know... you're a good man. Even if you are a monster."

Wick tried to hide his disappointment. Somehow, he had hoped for more.

"I mean to say..." Briar rolled her eyes. "You're sweet, alright? And thoughtful. And all sorts of other things that most people aren't. Nobody's protected me like you. Nobody looks out for me like you do."

She fell silent, biting her lip. She almost looked like

she regretted saying it, even as she pulled up a weak smile. "Is that what you wanted to hear?"

"Only if it was true."

Her smile wilted. She was obviously trying to drag it back up, but all her efforts failed. It made Wick feel conflicted. He wanted her to smile, of course, but not if she was using them as a shield to hide behind.

"It was," she admitted. "I wish it wasn't, but it was."

Wick frowned. "You... wish I treated you badly?"

"No," Briar scoffed, her eyes roving anywhere but him. "I just— I wish—"

She stammered to a stop. She was still shiny with sweat, smelling of desire and stress and his own come. Her shirt was half-laced, her breasts heaving as she panted.

"You wish," Wick prompted.

Briar's lips twitched bitterly. She shook her head and leaned up to touch his chest, her eyes falling half-lidded.

"I wish you would put your tongue inside me," she said huskily. "I didn't get to finish."

Wick knew he should have dropped to his knees and hoisted her legs over his shoulders. But he stayed there, spellbound as he watched her pink mouth go slack.

"Which hole?" Wick asked.

Briar shivered. "My... my cunt."

Wick nodded. But he couldn't tear his gaze from her lips. Her breathing was strange, almost erratic, as she stared up at him.

Wick thought of the mortals he'd seen kissing from a distance. Some of those kisses were quick and transactional, others were so deep and fond that they filled him with a longing he didn't fully understand.

Until now.

Wick leaned in.

Briar gasped. "Wait!"

Wick stopped. "What is it?"

Briar shook her head. Her head tilted, listening hard. "Do you hear that? If *I* can hear it, you must."

Wick concentrated. Distant birdsong, leaves on the cooling breeze, and behind it all, growing louder the more he listened:

"A waterfall," he said, surprised.

Briar's face lit up. "We're here!"

Wick frowned. "What do you mean?"

A cheery greeting drifted down from the trees. "Hello there!"

Wick dragged a wing in front of Briar automatically, only stopping when he looked up and saw the friendly smile on their intruder's face.

A woman around Briar's age stood on a high branch, spinning a staff energetically in one hand. Her hair was a tight black puff around her head, and she smelled of strange herbs and animal blood.

"Briar," said the stranger with an excited wave. "Good to see you! Why are you propositioning a naked Skullstalker?"

ELEVEN

Briar watched Wick's face, wishing she didn't care so much about his stupid reaction.

"See?" she said. "Waterfall. Surprise!"

"Surprise," Wick agreed in a tone that made her think that sometimes he just repeated her words when he didn't know what to say. It should have annoyed her. Instead, she was just annoyed at herself for how fond it made her.

Wick stared up at the waterfall with an unreadable expression. His whole body was still, no tail twitching or wings fidgeting. Just a complete, utter stillness that Briar had never known. It made her nervous. It made her jealous. It made her really pissed off that he could smell her damn emotions.

She pulled up a smile and tried to force the nerves out of her chest. "Pretty, right?"

"Pretty," Wick echoed. Then his tail flicked, and he

was back to normal. "Your witch picked a good place to live."

"Yeah, it's okay." Briar glanced back at Marigold's cottage, which was just as cozy and charming as the last time she was here, recovering from a gut wound.

The cottage was a round, quaint thing with wisteria dripping around the thinning roof and smoke piping merrily from the wonky brick chimney. It was worn down and in need of repair, but it was also one of the sweetest things Briar had ever seen. Like something from a story book. The kind of place where danger never touched you and you could sleep deeply every night, knowing all was right with your little world.

The kind of place, in other words, Briar could never stay. But she liked to visit from time to time.

One of the crooked cottage windows swung open, revealing Marigold wearing an apron and waving wildly.

"Are you two coming?" she called. "The tea's ready!"

"Coming," Briar yelled back.

She and Wick set off toward the cottage.

Wick leaned down to Briar. "What is 'tea?'"

"Hot, gross, brown water," Briar said. "Just force it down."

"Oh." Wick twisted back to look at the waterfall again. Briar marveled at him. How much nature had he seen in his endless Skullstalker years, and a waterfall could still make him go still like that?

"Why do you get like that?" she asked before she could stop herself. "First the mountains, now a waterfall. You go all quiet behind the eyes."

"I just like waterfalls," Wick replied. "The mountains are different."

"Different? How?"

Wick cocked his head. "I don't know."

He stopped, his gaze rising toward the mountains looming in the distance. For a moment, the stillness came over him again, strange and somehow less tranquil than the effect the waterfall had on him.

Then he shuddered all the way to his wingtips.

"Come," he said, turning back toward the cottage. "We have foul water to drink."

It was a short trip from the front door to the living room. And yet Wick managed to knock over a chair (tail), shatter a vase (wings), and swipe a painting off its hook (an unlucky elbow).

"I am sorry," he said as he sank into the lumpy couch. "I have never been inside a house before."

Briar giggled and sat down beside him. The couch was supposed to be big enough for four people, but Briar could barely wedge herself into the small space left beside Wick's bulk.

"Happens to the best of us," said Marigold cheerily. She set out a tray of tea on the table and sat down in an armchair across from them.

Briar nudged a table leg with her boot. It had several books stacked underneath it, just like when she had visited last time.

"So," Briar said. "Still no apothecary attached to this place."

Marigold sighed, balancing a teacup on a saucer. "I'm working on it! I just need one big job, and then I can finally hire some builders. And carpenters. And buy the starter supplies. And... oh, you know." Marigold smoothed out her skirt, which was always some kind of wrinkled. "So! We're friends with Skullstalkers now. Or... *more* than friends, I guess."

She gave Wick a judgy look. Which was better than rage and disgust, Briar reminded herself. Marigold wasn't a very judgy person, but Briar would have also been giving Wick the side-eye if their roles were reversed.

"He's different," Briar assured her. She patted Wick's wings, which were tucked in tightly behind his back. "He doesn't want to hurt anybody. That's actually one reason we want to talk to you."

Marigold's eyebrows shot up. "You're here for *him*?"

"No, *obviously* I'm here for me. For us," Briar said hurriedly. "We're cursed."

Marigold hummed into her teacup. "Another rocky misadventure with Briar Copperwood. What's the curse?"

Briar ground her teeth. "Remember Salaros? Wears special boots that make him tall, stinks like perfume—"

"Awful mustache," Marigold agreed. "I remember him. He died recently! That wasn't you, was it?"

"It was, actually. But only because he cursed me." Briar adjusted her shirt laces, which were stiff with sweat in a way that reminded her she needed to wash her clothes in that waterfall before bed. She felt oddly exposed, which was strange. Marigold had seen her in much worse states than standing rumpled in front of a naked man, like she'd seen in the clearing. But for some reason, she felt the urge to hide.

"I need to sleep with someone," Briar continued, her voice forcefully light. "Every day. Or my heart will burn up!"

Marigold made a face. "That's annoying. I guess you'd have to travel with someone! How did you end up with him?"

"He saved my life." Briar rubbed Wick's wing, already halfway through the movement before she noticed what she was doing. Then she realized how warm it sounded and cleared her throat, dropping her hand to her lap.

"We helped each other out," she corrected. "I told him about my curse, and he told me of his."

"I do not know if mine is a curse," Wick said. He was watching Briar's hand, the one that had been touching his wing. Then he cleared his throat, his head jerking around to Marigold.

"I have an uncontrollable blood frenzy," he explained.

"Ye-e-es," Marigold said, balancing a teacup on her knee. "You're a Skullstalker."

Briar pushed back another sting of annoyance. *You would have thought the same thing last week,* she reminded herself.

"It's not a Skullstalker *thing,*" she argued. "Wick says

it isn't normal for them. He can't control it. The others can."

"But I have *found* something that can," Wick said. He reached over and lifted the amulet around Briar's neck, his claws brushing Briar's collarbones. "This. The necklace you gave her. Whenever the blood frenzy starts, your necklace glows and makes it go away."

"Oh!" Marigold's smile shrank. Her eyes narrowed, and she leaned forward to examine the amulet.

Briar waited for her to speak. When the only thing that happened was that Marigold leaned further forward, Briar continued, "What did you make it out of?"

Marigold startled. "Huh? Oh! Well, I'll have to think about it. It was supposed to be for very basic magical protection..."

She trailed off. Her brows wrinkled, her mouth moving wordlessly as she went deeper and deeper into whatever magical theory she was falling into.

Luckily, Briar had witnessed enough deep dives to know how to snap Marigold out of it.

Briar leaned forward and snapped her fingers. "Marigold!"

Marigold jerked, tea splashing over her rumpled skirt.

"Gods!" Marigold brushed the tea away with a wince, then turned back to them with a lopsided smile. "Okay! Oooo*kay*. Salaros sex curse. Blood frenzy. We can assume which methods Salaros used; he always used the same ones for his curses... But a *blood frenzy*... And it's affected by the protection amulet..."

Marigold trailed off again, her mouth moving around

complicated magic theory that Briar used to sit through for hours at a time while she tuned her out.

Then she straightened, clicking her saucer and teacup onto the table with such enthusiasm that another tide of tea washed over the side.

"Can I look inside your head?" she asked Wick, wiping her hands clean. "It will only take a moment. I have a theory."

Wick looked over at Briar, alarmed.

Briar squeezed his knee comfortingly. "Marigold's a great witch. You don't have to worry."

Wick's tail swished anxiously around his legs. But he gave Marigold a brisk nod, leaning toward her when she beckoned him.

"Just a peek," Marigold assured him distractedly. She had that intense look she always got when she was pouring all her attention into her magic. Her eyes were bright and flinty, her friendly face dropping into a narrow-minded focus that made Briar think back to all those times Marigold's magic had saved their lives when they were children, mostly by getting them food. Levitation spells on a pie on a windowsill or a brief invisibility spell to let Briar dart into a butcher's shop and grab a ham hock, both of which left Marigold stumbling and woozy as they made their escape.

There was no wooziness in Marigold now. Only a single-minded intensity that got more powerful the longer she stared into Wick's fiery eyes.

"Huh," Marigold whispered.

Then her eyes went flat white. Wick's eyes followed

suit, and then they both sat up ramrod straight as their minds connected.

Briar shifted uneasily. She hadn't lied to Wick: Marigold *was* a great witch. But there was something spooky about watching her do this type of magic. Levitation and invisibility were one thing. Connecting two minds was another.

Especially when it was Wick. For all his sweetness, there was that untamable rage hiding inside of him. She almost expected him and Marigold to leap up with twin roars, their eyes flashing with fire.

But they stayed there, sitting eerily straight with those milky white eyes, just long enough for Briar to start to sweat.

Then they both jerked, their eyes going back to normal as they sagged forward.

Briar touched Wick's back between his wings. "Wick! Hey, are you alright?"

"I am fine," he said, breathing raggedly. He looked over at Briar, and she wondered when his fiery eyes became so comforting.

Marigold wheezed out a laugh, fanning her face. She was sweating, drops appearing on her hairline.

"That was new," she said with nervous delight. She grabbed her wet teacup, her hand shaking as she sipped. "I-I can cure you. Cure you both, even. And the best news is, I only need one more ingredient for both of those spells!"

"Great," Briar said. "What is it?"

Marigold grimaced. "That... might be a problem. It's

just up in the mountains, but I don't have time to go up there right now. I'm behind on some ritual translations for my clients, and I promised I would finish them this week."

"We can do it," Briar said eagerly. "Right? Wick can fly; it makes travel so much easier!"

Marigold brightened, clutching her tea with shaking hands. "I didn't think about that! That's so helpful. Well, if you go up the mountains and get me the flower I need, I can cure you both within the day."

Briar clasped Wick's knee excitedly. "Do you hear that? We're so close! What flower?"

"I'll show you! Here, it's in my library." Marigold stood, brushing her wet skirt once more as she turned toward the hallway.

Briar stood. Wick stood with her and immediately knocked over the table with his swishing tail.

"Damn," he blurted. "I am sorry."

He bent down to turn it back on its feet. His wings knocked into a bookcase, knocking over a stack of books and a framed sketch of the mountains that waited in the distance.

"Sorry," he repeated, grabbing at everything he was knocking over.

Marigold stopped in the mouth of the hallway to give him a strained smile. "How about you stay in here for now? Briar, come and see this flower."

Briar held back a smirk and turned to Wick. "Maybe just sit back down, big boy."

Wick paused, halfway through bending down to pick

up the books, like he was deciding whether it was best to try to fix this and risk knocking over more things or sit quietly on the couch where none of his limbs could break more of this tiny cottage.

Briar glanced back as she left the room to see Wick sitting down slowly on the couch.

Marigold was on Briar as soon as she stepped into the cramped library.

"*Briar*," she hissed, her smile twisting with shock and disbelief. "A Skullstalker? *Really*? Gods, does he even *fit*?"

"Mostly," Briar said with a confidence she didn't fully feel. She rubbed her thighs together, both her holes twinging from so much stretching. Her panties were wet with his come, yet again. Maybe he could make good on what he'd said in the clearing and lick it out of her before they found someplace to sleep.

Briar looked around the narrow library, full of towering stacks of books in various stages of decay.

"When you start up your apothecary," she began. "Are you going to do a discount for old friends?"

"Don't change the subject," Marigold warned. She even looked like she meant it, right up until her mouth twitched.

Briar giggled. Marigold tried not to join in, but her mouth kept twitching until she was joining in, the two of them falling over each other laughing like they were young girls again.

"Gods," Marigold repeated, wiping her eyes. They were bloodshot, Briar noted. It almost looked like flames were circling her irises.

"But really," Marigold continued. "A Skullstalker. I didn't even know they could sleep with humans!"

"Me neither. But I found out."

Marigold's face twisted. "I couldn't do it. He has a skull face!"

"Only half of it," Briar said defensively. She went to lean back against a stack of books, then immediately thought better of it when the stack started to tilt. She turned back to Marigold, whose hands were up, ready to catch the stack if it fell.

Briar swallowed. If there was anyone in the world she could tell about her stupid, soft feelings, it was Marigold. Her only true friend in the world.

"He's actually pretty wonderful," Briar began. "He's sweet. He's... good. I know he's a Skullstalker, but I think he's truly a good creature."

Marigold blinked. She looked expectant, like she was expecting Briar to come in at the last second with a joke. In her defense, it sounded like something Briar would do.

Briar laughed self-consciously and stepped away from the stack of books teetering behind her. "So. You had a flower to show me?"

"What? Oh." Marigold rushed over to the corner of the room and heaved out a giant tome. She hauled it open, flicking water-stained pages until she reached one with a detailed sketch of a dappled rose with pointed petals.

"It's called the snowskull rose," she explained, holding the book out. "It grows in small clusters up in the mountains. The locals will be able to give you directions."

"Locals?" Briar had assumed they wouldn't run into anyone. "People *live* up there? I thought those were rumors."

"There's a whole town," Marigold said. "They're a bit... *weird*. But they aren't hostile."

"Weird," Briar repeated. "Weird how?"

"Oh, nothing too bad. It's mostly their magic practices, to be honest. Their magic is very, um, intimate."

Briar grinned. "*Intimate*? Do you mean sex magic?"

"I try not to know," Marigold admitted.

She tore the flower page out of the book and handed it to Briar, who studied it carefully. It had no color, but there were notes in the margins: the center was white, almost in the shape of a skull. The rest of it was pure black.

Marigold heaved the book back onto a shelf. It wobbled, and they both froze until the shelf stilled.

"I'll try not to stumble into any more weird sex magic," Briar said as she tucked the piece of paper into her pocket. "So, how does it work? The protection amulet, I mean. I didn't expect it to protect me from wayward Skullstalkers."

"It doesn't. The Skullstalker—*Wick's* case is unique." Marigold eyed the amulet around Briar's neck, gnawing on her lip thoughtfully.

"Why?" Briar asked. "What links this amulet to his blood frenzy? What sort of magic is it?"

Marigold startled. She laughed nervously, and Briar noticed that she was still sweating, a line of salt running down the side of her face.

"Oh, that's—" She waved a dismissive hand. It looked strange, Briar noticed. Chapped and red and worn, like she had been out in the cold for many days in a row.

"It would take too long to explain," Marigold said. "You always get bored by magic theory. What matters is that it will work!"

"You seem confident," Briar noted. "I thought you'd never dealt with this before."

"I haven't." Marigold pushed her sweaty hair out of her face. "But like you said, I'm a great witch."

She smiled, sunny and enthusiastic in that way that Briar used to hate before she realized Marigold wasn't faking it.

Briar started to smile back, then she stopped.

For a moment, Marigold's eyes were slate white once more. Something spun in the center of them, thick as a snowstorm. But before Briar could panic, Marigold blinked, and her eyes were back to normal again.

"I'll get you sorted, Briar. Don't you worry." Marigold patted her shoulder with those oddly chapped hands, then turned toward the hall. "I'll get your room set up. I still have your favorite blanket! And some spare clothes, if you want to change."

"Thanks," Briar said, plucking at her sweaty clothes. Then she paused. "Hey. About that room..."

TWELVE

The witch's spare room faced the waterfall.

Wick watched water pour into the river and thought about the phrase. *Spare room.* According to Briar, it was a room where visitors could sleep.

"Or a place to keep your gold," Briar added as she jumped up onto the bed next to him. "I think I'll have a few gold rooms when I have my own place."

Wick turned away from the window to watch her. She was wearing the "sleep clothes" Marigold had given her: a linen shirt and a soft pair of underclothes. Every time she moved, the shirt rose and exposed her belly. Wick wanted to kiss it very badly.

"They'll have to be hidden rooms, of course," Briar continued, sitting up beside him with her soft stomach showing in the moonlight. "Can't let anybody see where I keep my important things. That's how you get robbed."

"Of course," said Wick, who had never had to worry

about getting robbed at any moment of his long existence. Even animals stayed away from him and his territory. Something in their bones told them he was a threat.

Wick decided he would like a spare room. The more he stayed in a house, the more he enjoyed it. It would have to be bigger than this, of course. Or less full of things. He had the feeling that he could move around quite freely if they moved the clutter. He could pile his nest into one of the rooms and have others for guests.

Briar butted her forehead against his shoulder. "You're quiet. What's going on in that big, horned head of yours?"

Wick grunted. His head was still throbbing from Marigold's spell. It had been strange having someone rooting around in his head.

"Marigold," he said. "You said she is a witch. Not a warlock."

Briar leaned back, frowning. "I did. Why?"

"She doesn't have a patron?"

"No," Briar said with a curious smile. "She thought about becoming a warlock when we were teenagers, then decided it was too risky. Always at the whim of your patron, and what have you. Why?"

Wick shook his head. It still ached—an odd, scratchy feeling that reminded him of whenever he had to stick his fingers into his wounds and pull out debris.

But more importantly, it also felt *familiar*. Which made no sense if it was just Marigold, the mortal witch, probing into his head. It still did not make much sense if it was a god or demon she was pledged to, but at least

Wick had *met* gods and demons before. He had never met Marigold. She could never have produced this cold, deep familiarity that still lingered long after the spell ended.

There was only one thing that could. But that, too, was impossible.

"Never mind," he said, then paused. "Has anyone told you about the Titans?"

Briar propped herself up on her elbows, gazing up at him so sweetly he was tempted to forgo his explanation and kiss her senseless.

"No," she said. "Who are they?"

Wick hesitated. It *was* impossible. But in the moment before Marigold released him, it had been there, freezing and unmistakable, a strange voice half-remembered from dreams. And for once, that voice hadn't been coming from inside his own head.

"They existed before the Skullstalkers," Wick said. "Impossibly large giants made of rock. Some of my brothers claim they *created* the Skullstalkers."

Briar's eyes lit up joyfully. "Is this your creation myth? I didn't know you had one."

"It is no myth. It is real."

"Of course," Briar said, nodding sagely. "I've just never heard of them, is all."

"They did not stray to the mortal realm," Wick said, trying to remember all that Slate had told him. "Except in the final days. They were fighting amongst each other. That is how they died out, and this age began."

He paused. Briar nudged his shoulder.

"Don't stop," she said. "You were obviously about to say something exciting. Will they rise again?"

"No," Wick said slowly. "As I said, they are dead. But... some of us hear whispers. Icy songs in our heads. Most of my brothers say it is nonsense. But others claim they hear it."

Briar's teasing smile dimmed. "Oh? Do you hear your makers, Wick?"

Wick stayed silent. The voice had been clearer than any whispers he'd heard in dreams, then half-forgotten. His brother Slate had assured him it was nothing more than sleep. But he had never heard those strange whispers, as deep in him as his blood. Maybe even deeper.

"Wick?" Briar repeated.

Wick squeezed his eyes shut, banishing all thoughts of Titans from his mind. He had an end to the blood frenzy in sight, a waterfall outside the window, and Briar next to him. All was well.

"I am enjoying the waterfall," he said, turning to watch it pour. "I will have a window like this in my nest room."

Briar's uncertainty faded, replaced by a blazing grin. She pressed closer to him, dropping her chin into his chest.

"Will you now? What else will you have in this waterfall home?"

"Less things to knock over," he replied. "And a spare room for when you come to visit."

Briar's head snapped up. She stared at him like she

was searching for evidence of a joke. Then her eyes soft-
ened, and she dropped her chin back onto him again.

"Sure, big boy," she said quietly. "I'd like that."

Then she looked away, bouncing in place on the bed.
It creaked ominously.

"Still holding up," Briar said happily. "Told you it
wouldn't break."

Wick nodded. He didn't dare move. Every shift made
the bed whine in protest.

"Still. Suppose we shouldn't make too much trouble," Briar continued thoughtfully. She bit her lip, as if
she were thinking hard. Then she turned to him with a
smile that almost reached her eyes, her mouth opening in
a yawn that turned genuine halfway through.

"I guess I *am* tired," she admitted, rubbing her eyes.
"Another big, strange day with the gentleman Skullstalker will tire anyone out."

"Yes," Wick agreed mindlessly. He settled carefully
into the bed, the wood creaking with every small movement, and gathered Briar into his arms.

Briar hesitated, as she always did. Then she leaned
into him.

Moonlight streamed into the room. It was colder
here, near the mountains. Briar was rubbing her arms
more than usual.

"Wick?" she whispered.

Wick looked down at her expectantly, waiting for her
to say something about another blanket, or that he
should cover her more thoroughly.

Briar bit her lip. "Can I try something?"

"Of course," Wick said.

She pushed herself up on his chest and leaned over him. She smelled sour, like she was worried about something.

Wick frowned. "Briar?"

Briar leaned down and kissed him.

Wick's eyes stayed open. He could see her perfectly, even though the moonlight did not reach her face: her sweet blonde brow, furrowed with concentration. Her pale lashes brushed his cheek. So close and so small and perfect, her lips parting on a sigh as he kissed her back cautiously.

He was clumsy. He knew it. But Briar's lips were slow and gentle, and soon Wick's eyes drifted shut.

The sour scent faded from the bedroom air. Another scent replaced it, soft and contented, which usually only occurred when she was falling asleep in his arms.

She touched his face. Her thumb brushed the place where bone became skin, trailing down to touch a scar dimpling his cheek. Her touch felt bigger than the blow that had given him the scar in the first place.

Wick made a noise in her mouth. Not a growl, a lost animal moan.

Briar pulled back. At first, Wick thought she was startled. Then he saw her face; there was no shock on it. He could not actually tell what was on it, and her scent was a jumble once more.

"What was that for?" Wick managed.

"I just wanted..." Briar cleared her throat, giving him

an odd smile. "I wanted to see what it was like. Not everybody gets the chance to kiss a Skullstalker."

Wick waited. "Did you enjoy it?"

"I did." Briar ducked her head, flustered. "Gods, that was your first kiss, wasn't it?"

"It was wonderful," Wick assured her.

Briar flushed. It was strange to see her be so affected over a kiss after all the things they had done together.

"Good. You deserve..." She stopped, biting her lip. "Goodnight, big boy."

She lay down in his arms and hid her face from him. Wick stroked her back through her sleep shirt, listened to the waterfall pour, and did something he had not done before—he prayed. He did not pledge himself to any deity in particular; Skullstalkers were not a religious bunch, and most gods would not hear them anyway. But he sent his thoughts out across the voids, hoping against hope they would be heard.

Please, he prayed. *Let me keep this peace. I would give anything.*

He expected nothing back, and he received it.

Except for the smallest whisper when he was on the verge of sleep. A cold, strange stab at the edge of his mind:

Come home, it whispered.

<h1 style="text-align:center">THIRTEEN</h1>

"There," Marigold panted, stepping back to admire her work. "What do you think?"

Briar looked up at Wick, who was shaking the magic shimmers from his hair.

Because he had *hair* now. A proper head of it. The illusion of it, anyway. Along with the illusion of a shirt, pants, and even shoes, with mortal proportions to fill them out. Marigold had pointed out that they would never get past the locals with a Skullstalker and had given Wick a glamor spell to ease the way.

Wick cocked his head expectantly. "Well?"

Briar hummed. He made for a handsome human, if you liked that sort of thing. But he also looked quite... bland. Especially his eyes, which were dull brown. Briar missed the fire. And the top half of his face looked naked without the skull fused to it. He was still very tall, but nowhere near as tall as he was a minute ago.

"You look great," she lied. She nodded at his back,

which looked deceivingly wingless with Marigold's glamor spell. "You can still get us up the mountain, right?"

"I can." Air displaced around Wick, and Briar imagined those invisible wings flapping.

"Then it's perfect." Briar patted down her borrowed clothes—another laced-up shirt and pants that were only slightly too baggy—and turned to Marigold. "Thanks. Really lowered our chance of getting attacked by angry townsfolk."

"That's the aim!" Marigold wiped sweat away from her brow and grinned, spinning her staff. "Safe travels, you two. Still have the sketch?"

Briar patted her pocket where the flower sketch resided. "Got it."

"Good," Marigold said. "I hope the locals aren't too strange."

"I promise not to get dragged into any magic sex rituals," Briar said sarcastically.

Marigold's laugh was less certain than Briar would like. Then she hugged Briar, who hugged back tightly. Marigold was the only person she could hug without reminding herself where her weapons were hidden.

She let herself sink into the embrace of an old friend. Sweet, familiar, and...

Cold? Briar frowned and leaned back. Marigold looked flushed, spots of color high on her cheeks. But that cheek had been icy where it had pressed into Briar's neck.

Marigold blinked. "What? Do I have something on my face?"

"You're *freezing*," Briar said.

"I am?" Marigold patted her forehead with a titter. "Must be all this mountain air! Well, have a nice flight! I'm a little jealous I have to stay here and work. I bet no mortal has ever had a Skullstalker fly them anywhere. Unless it was to eat them, obviously."

"Most Skullstalkers do not have wings," Wick pointed out.

"Right! Of course." Marigold spun her staff, a nervous gesture she had picked up since she had been given her very first one in childhood. "Anywho, have fun! Don't get murdered."

"As long as your glamor holds up, that won't be a problem." Briar stepped close to Wick and let him scoop her up in his arms.

The glamor flickered. But just for a moment, and only when her face brushed Wick's chest. In that instant, he towered above her, horned and beautiful. Then she blinked, and the illusion was back in place, a boring mortal staring down at her.

"Whoo," Marigold said, her voice high. "That's... intimate."

"What do you expect me to do, cling to his back? That's where his wings are." Briar flicked Marigold a salute. "Have fun with your theories."

"I always do!"

Briar patted Wick's chest. "Take me for a fly, big boy."

Wick took off. Marigold waved, big and goofy, both hands raised. Briar laughed and waved back, watching the forest blur around them.

Briar grabbed for Wick's shirt, laughing when her hands slid against bare skin.

"Your clothes look so real," she said as they soared above the trees. "How does it feel?"

"Strange," Wick replied. "Like there is less of me."

"It sure looks like it." Briar looked up sadly at his skull-less face, those boring normal teeth behind his lips. She had been so terrified of his monstrous features when they first met—his fangs, his hulking height, his fiery eyes—and now she was missing them.

She looked away, worried he would catch something embarrassing in her expression. Then she cursed and tried desperately to reign in her emotions, which he could fucking *smell*. She was never going to get used to that.

With another powerful beat of his invisible wings, Wick broke the tree line.

Briar stared at the mountains looming overhead. They were grey and oddly savage looking, cruel points twisting into the cold air.

"I didn't realize they were so close," Briar said.

Wick didn't respond. He was staring up at the mountains, something faraway in his eyes.

Briar cleared her throat uneasily. "We'll need to find somewhere warm for you to take care of my curse."

"Yes," Wick said after a moment. His arms tightened

around her, and for a moment, Briar thought she had caught a spark of fire in his eyes.

"We will do that as soon as we find the town," Wick continued.

Briar rubbed her chest. The curse was barely a flicker this early in the morning. But she could still feel it if she focused—a small, dangerous ember glowing behind her ribs.

"Fly fast," she said.

Wick let out a concerned rumble. "Why? Are you in pain?"

"No, just..." Briar swallowed. There was no casual way to admit she wanted the comforting weight of him on top of her, his impossible cock stretching her out. He might look different with the glamor, but there would be no mistaking what he truly was when he was fucking her.

"I just like getting it out of the way for the day," she said.

Wick said nothing. When she risked a glance up, his eyes were fixed on the mountain.

Yedzeva was a small village on the southernmost edge of the mountain. There was a snowy cliff hanging over it, casting them in shadow for most of the day. And they did *not* like strangers.

"State your purpose," barked a guard at the village entrance.

Briar blinked. His accent was strange, thick and

twisted in a way that made her think of other lands—but none she'd heard of.

Wick looked expectantly at Briar, who smiled easily and linked their arms together.

"My husband and I are looking for a room for the night," Briar said. "We wanted to pass straight through the mountain, but our carriage got stuck. Do you have a room available? We'll take anything, truly."

She rubbed her and Wick's arms, trying to look as sad as possible.

The guard grunted. Then he jerked his head, standing aside.

"Don't cause any trouble," he warned.

"Us? Never." Briar gave him a grateful smile and then dragged Wick with her over the village border to the snowy path leading uphill. She waited until the guard was out of sight, then tossed Wick a wink. "What did I tell you? I can talk my way into anything."

"I believe it." Wick paused. Then, delightfully clumsy, he winked back at her.

Briar cackled. Then they reached the top of the hill and stopped. Yedzeva lay ahead: a cramped collection of houses around a town square full of snow and stalls and people dressed in thick robes, walking very fast.

"Move," said a woman brusquely as she shoved Briar out of the way.

Briar stepped back and watched her go. She was hunched over a basket of dried fruits, looking incredibly stressed. She also had the same thick accent as the guard.

They really are isolated up here, Briar thought. She

watched the townsfolk with their heads down, discomfort brewing in her gut. For all her joking with Marigold about sex magic, she had been expecting something more welcoming.

"Come on." She led Wick toward the town square.

He got stiffer with every step. Briar frowned, looking up to see him watching the townsfolk with a panicked expression.

"I do not like crowds," he explained.

Briar winced. Crowds and blood frenzies didn't mix.

"Yeah, I bet," she muttered. She pulled him out of the way of a speed-walking man, who gave them one glance before stumbling to a stop.

"Cor," the man said, gaping up at Wick and exposing all three of his teeth. "You're as tall as a Skullstalker!"

"Skullstalkers are much bigger," Wick said hastily.

The man grunted in disbelief and then kept walking, his head down.

Briar pulled her coat tighter and looked around. That man wasn't the only one giving Wick strange looks; everyone who bothered to look up was lingering on them now. Briar supposed they didn't get many visitors, what with their isolated location and inhospitable welcome at the border.

Wick let out a blustery breath. Something smacked into Briar's leg, and she could only tell by the feel that it was his tail swishing back and forth in worry.

"We're okay," Briar whispered, rubbing his arm genuinely this time. "Nobody's attacking you."

"It is not me I am worried about," Wick said. He

stared around the town square like he was imagining tearing through it in a bloody fury.

Briar squeezed his arm. "Hey. Cut that out. Tell me about the waterfall house you're going to get when you're cured."

It took a second. But Wick tore his eyes away from the town and looked at her with those boring human eyes that made her miss those flames swimming in black.

"It is not a waterfall house," he started. "It is a house near a waterfall. I want to see it from my bedroom window. I would like a bedroom. A nest room, I suppose. And... a room for you to stay."

He said it cautiously, like he wanted to say something else. Briar knew what *she* wanted to say: would he sleep next to her when she visited? Why couldn't she just curl up beside him in his nest? Her curse would be over, to be sure. But it didn't have to mean they were over.

Right?

"I have not thought about much else," Wick admitted.

Briar forced herself to stop thinking about falling asleep beside him a year from now, two years, *ten*, and patted his glamored chest, which was actually his stomach.

"Let's go ask about a room," she said. Then she paused. "Wait. Let's ask about the flowers first, *then* the room. Might as well get them both done at once."

Wick nodded. His shoulders were still up around his ears, but his tail wasn't whacking into her anymore.

Briar looked around. The only person who wasn't

charging through the town square with their head down or standing behind a stall yelling about mostly fresh meat was an elderly woman sitting on a bench at the other side of the square. She was covered in so many robes that Briar could hardly see her face.

Briar led Wick over and gave the old woman a polite wave. "Hello! My husband and I heard about some beautiful flowers we can find in your town. Could you point us in the right direction? They look like this."

She took Marigold's sketch out of her pocket.

The elderly woman stared at it. She was so hunched it made Briar wince in sympathy. The robes couldn't help, Briar thought as she looked at the layers upon layers of robes piled over the woman's head and shoulders. Interestingly, the last layer was a thin golden mesh she hadn't noticed until they got close.

"They are past the forsaken ravine at the edge of town," the woman croaked. "It belongs to the mountain. We do not go there."

"Oh." Briar glanced up at Wick, who gave her a look that meant that no matter how forsaken it was, the ravine was easy enough to fly over.

"Hear that, honey? There go our flower dreams! Ah, well, thanks anyway." Briar inclined her head and even gave the old woman a little curtsey, hoping she came off as an endearing foreigner unfamiliar with their customs instead of a dangerous idiot stranger who needed to be run out of town as fast as possible.

"Another question, if that's alright," Briar continued with a simpering little smile that she brought out when she wanted someone to think she wasn't a threat. "My husband and I are looking for somewhere to stay tonight. Does this town have an inn? Or even just a room? We'll only be the one night."

The old woman stared. Not at her, Briar realized with a start, but at Wick.

Briar wished she could nudge him. Wick was the opposite of non-threatening, looming over everyone, even *with* the glamor. Even if he didn't, he was so stiff he set Briar on edge just looking at him.

The old woman's eyes widened. She pushed her robes off her head and rose, clutching a twisting cane in her unsteady hands as she stared at them.

Briar looked up at Wick, who looked back at her in panic. Could this old woman see past the glamor? Were they about to get found out?

"Or we can just leave," Briar said, sensing trouble. "If there is no room. You folks probably don't get many visitors—"

The old woman cut her off. "My prediction has come to pass!"

The town square stilled. All the townsfolk who had been bustling past with their robes around their faces stopped and stared.

Briar stepped closer to Wick warily. Something brushed her other arm, and Briar forced herself not to react as Wick's invisible wing closed around her protectively.

"Don't do anything until I say," Briar whispered. "There's a lot of them, we don't want—"

The old woman cut her off again, her hands flinging out under her heavy robes.

"The couple who will fulfill the annual ritual has finally arrived," she cried.

Briar stopped. *That* wasn't what she had been expecting.

The old woman struggled toward them, every step an effort.

"It has been foretold," she whispered. "Once a year, the mountain must be appeased. Finally, you come!"

"Ha ha," Briar said loudly, unable to muster a real laugh yet. "What ritual are you talking about? No virgin sacrifices, I hope?"

"Void, no. Nothing like that."

Briar sagged with relief. Wick's wing loosened around her.

"You only have to join together in body," the old woman continued. "In front of the town. As the ritual commands."

Huh, Briar thought. *Guess I wasn't joking about the sex magic after all. Could've used a bigger heads-up, Marigold.*

"Join together in body," Wick repeated. "You mean we must mate?"

"You must join together until he spills inside you," the old woman said. "And appease the mountain."

Briar twisted to see the townsfolk around her. None of them *looked* like perverts who wanted to watch them fuck, but she'd been wrong about that sort of thing before. Briar started, "I don't think—"

"You will be richly rewarded," the old woman said over her. "As the ritual commands."

"I should consult my husband," Briar announced.

She dragged Wick away and lowered her voice, all too aware of how many eyes were on them. "What are we thinking? And why do none of these things ever care about *me* finishing?"

"It is an oversight," Wick agreed. "I heard you talk to your witch of sex magic. I thought you were joking."

"I *was*," Briar hissed. "Marigold just said their magic was 'intimate!' That could've meant anything!"

She looked around the town again, her skin pricking with goosebumps under her thick robes. She hoped that wherever the ritual happened was heated.

"You wish to do it," Wick said slowly.

"Of course, I want to do it! They said I'd be richly rewarded!" Briar beamed. "I'm never going to see any of these mountain weirdos again. Why not fuck in front of them? And save them from the... mountain's wrath, or whatever they think will happen if they don't make strangers fuck in front of them once a year."

Wick grunted. "Then I will do it."

"Great!" Briar clapped his arms, then paused. Wick was still stiff under her touch, and not in a fun way. "Are... are you sure? You don't have to."

Wick frowned. "I can do it. As long as the glamor holds."

"Yeah, good point." Briar thought about it. They would ideally need to do this sooner rather than later for the glamor to hold.

She turned back to the old woman. "When does this ritual happen?"

"When the sun is at its peak," the old woman rasped. She pointed at the sky, where the sun was mostly blocked by the giant cliff in the way.

"Okay," Briar said. "That works."

Fourteen

This seems like a poor place to build a village, Wick thought as he stared out the window at the looming cliff. The sun was hidden behind it completely, casting a huge shadow that covered the entire village of Yedzeva.

Wick turned to the mortal man who had just finished smearing him with strange-smelling mud. "What happens if you do not appease the mountain each year?"

The mortal bowed his head as he cleaned mud off his hands. "The cliff over our town will fall and crush us all."

Wick grunted. For all he had enjoyed Marigold's house—except for the clutter he kept knocking over—this village was not making him want to spend time here.

"When can I see Briar?" he asked.

The mortal frowned. "You cannot! Not until the ritual."

"Oh," said Wick. "Of course."

The mortal forced the frown off his face and dropped

his muddy cloth in a bowl. "Forgive me, stranger. I forget myself. I should know that heathens such as yourself do not know of our beloved and wrathful mountain."

"That's alright," Wick said, pleased. He could get used to mortals making conversation rather than running in terror. The more it happened, the more he liked it.

The mortal did something Briar had called a "bow" earlier. "I will leave you in peace. Madame Thatchbore will be with you soon to lead you to the ritual."

He did another small bow and left. Wick watched the door close and then stood there, waiting. The mortal had warned him not to smudge the markings over his face and chest.

Wick ghosted his hand over the markings, not daring to touch. Not for the first time, he wished he had paid attention when his older brother Slate told him about magic. Since Wick had no ability for it, he had never bothered to listen. More fool he—another phrase Briar had taught him on their strange journey.

The door creaked open. Wick turned toward it, expecting the man to come back in, glaring at him for almost touching the markings.

Briar entered instead. She was wearing a hooded fur robe and not much else, her ankles pale with cold. She also had mud streaked over her in the same odd, pointy markings as he did.

"Hey," she whispered with a grin, adjusting the hood over her head. "How are you feeling?"

Wick cocked his head. "They let you out? They did not let *me* out."

"They don't know I'm out," Briar said.

Wick nodded. That made sense.

He plucked at his loincloth, which she would see as pants. "How long does your witch's glamor last?"

"For a human? A few days, usually. But on a Skull-stalker? Good question." Briar went to rub her face, then stopped just before she could smear the mud.

"Damn stuff," she muttered, poking her skin between the markings. "At least it dried fast. Now come on, we don't have much time."

"Time?"

Briar nodded and sat down in a rickety chair in the corner. She poked her legs out of the robe, long and bare.

"You need to get me ready," Briar explained. "You know how much stretching I need. So you can slide in easily when we're out there saving these freaky townsfolk from their big, bad mountain."

Something cold and rocky itched inside Wick's head. He ignored it and got on his knees, inhaling Briar's hot, eager scent as he pulled her other leg out from underneath the fur robe.

Briar let go of the robe. It fell away to reveal her naked body, spirals of mud decorating her soft belly. She also took a knife out of her sleeve, placing it down on the ground before straightening up.

"Careful with the mud," she breathed.

Wick nuzzled her thigh and breathed in. Her scent was stronger now, stronger than the mud on her body and the snow waiting outside.

"Hurry," she told him, biting her lip against a smile.

She was enjoying this, Wick realized. Just as they had both enjoyed, in some strange way, being fucked against a tree while they had to stay quiet for the hunters. He wondered if she would enjoy being ritually mated in front of this small village.

He did not yet know if he would. The idea made him feel prickly and possessive. But mostly, he was worried about getting attacked. Having mortals around usually meant he was about to get a crossbow pointed at him. Mating with so many mortals around him did not sound appealing. But he would not say no to Briar.

Especially if the mountain's wrath was real. He did not particularly like this village, but he would prefer not to see it crushed.

He slid his tongue up Briar's thigh, watching it turn shiny under his touch. It made him wonder what she would look like covered in his come. What she would *smell* like.

Wick pushed the tip of his tongue inside her.

Briar groaned, working her hips against him. She reached up to touch her breasts, then grimaced. "Ugh. Stupid mud."

Wick looked up to see her twisting her nipples carefully. Usually, she would be squeezing them, but there was mud circling her nipples.

"Come on," she urged.

Wick pushed his tongue deeper. Her slick flesh parted around him, squeezing his tongue eagerly.

"*Yes.*" Briar tipped her head back, resting against the fur draped over her chair. "Stretch me out, sweetheart."

Something warm curled inside Wick's chest. Soft and gentle, nothing like the dangerous haze of the blood frenzy. It had been happening more and more with Briar's pet names. It felt less like she was trying to be charming, as with the wink, and more like she was truly fond of him. Friends, just like they agreed.

Perhaps even more than that.

Briar clutched his horns. Her eyes flew open, her head coming up to watch him.

"This is so strange," she said. "I can't see them, but I can feel them."

Wick rumbled, thrusting his tongue deeper. His mouth pooled with spit, and he had to fight the urge to plunge his tongue as far as it could go. He always wanted more with Briar: to hold her down, to take, to *devour*. His primal impulses had never been so fun until she showed up.

"I miss them," Briar continued.

Wick looked up, surprised. He had assumed that his monstrous traits were tolerated, nothing more. But there was nothing fake in Briar's expression, her eyes falling shut in bliss as he worked inside her.

"Good to have something to grab onto," Briar continued. Her legs jerked around him as he laved at that sweet bump inside her that never failed to make her writhe. "A-and your tail. Like when it wraps around my leg when you're fucking me. Like you can't get enough— *oh*!"

She trailed off in a gasp as he pressed forward, the end of his skull mask bumping into her clit.

"*That's* it," Briar said with a victorious grin. "Am I getting loose enough for you? Can I take your cock yet?"

Wick growled, gripping her thighs even more tightly. His cock pulsed under his loincloth, already leaking from the thought of sinking into her hot, wet warmth. She was always so tight, no matter how much he stretched her beforehand. Always squeezing down around his cock so beautifully, stretching around his girth.

He pulled his tongue out, ignoring her moan of protest. It faded into a satisfied sigh as he slipped his fingers in—two of them, claws carefully retracted, curling up against that bump that made her spasm around him.

"Gods," she gasped. "Oh, gods."

She rocked her hips against him. The chair squeaked.

Wick held her still. "Hush. They will hear."

"They'll hear much more of me once that ritual starts," Briar said with a grin.

Wick pushed a third finger inside. Briar's grin opened in another gasp, her neck arching into a straight line so tantalizing Wick wanted to bite it.

"Hush," Wick repeated.

He reached up and slid his fingers into her mouth. Briar's eyes flew open, bright with surprise. Then she went lax. Her lips sealed around his fingers, sucking eagerly and muffling moans as he fingered her.

Wick's hips moved against nothing. He wanted to mate her right there, ritual be damned. He wanted to see how far she could take him, wanted to turn her over and have her other hole again, wanted to shove into her mouth and fill her up from every angle—

The door opened.

"Void take me," said the man who had smeared mud on him before.

The elderly woman stood beside him, looking remarkably unbothered as she clutched her cane.

Briar spat out Wick's fingers reluctantly and beamed.

"Madame Thatchbore," she said, before bending down to grab her knife from the ground, passing off the movement as a method to hide her naked body. "Lovely to see you."

"Save that for the altar," Madame Thatchbore replied. She stepped back, nodding at the village, made dark by the towering cliff. "Come. It is time."

They led Wick and Briar down a snowy path to a circular altar. It was brushed clean and studded with candles, wax melting down and puddling onto the stone.

"So much for heat," Briar said, adjusting her fur robe. "You'll have to keep me warm, big boy."

Wick did not reply. He stared around at the people gathered to watch. They were dressed in robes similar to the old woman's, all of them clutching candles. It was an oddly eerie sight, made all the eerier by the scent of anticipation in the air.

Briar gasped. "Look."

Wick followed her gaze. There, beyond the altar, stood a ravine. It was narrower than Wick had expected, but cracked and jagged like a broken bone. A series of twisting cliffs waited on the other side, lined with the flowers Wick recognized from the sketch. There was only a glimpse of them before they vanished into the spiraling cliffs, which blocked the rest of the flowers from view.

"We'll have to come back after everyone's gone," Briar whispered as they approached the altar at the edge of the ravine.

Wick nodded. He stared at the twisting cliffs beyond the ravine. It was no wonder the mortals had invented a myth to be afraid of them. Those cliffs looked like the perfect place to get lost.

Briar cleared her throat, worry clear in her scent even if it wasn't in her face. "Hey, Madame Thatchbore. You were saying something about being richly rewarded?"

Madame Thatchbore nodded and waved a gnarled hand at the crowd.

The crowd parted. The mud mortal stepped through, carrying a large bowl of golden coins and goblets. They looked old and—for some reason—familiar.

"Gifts from deep within the mountain," Madame Thatchbore declared as the mud mortal placed the bowl onto a stone pillar. "We give unto you, for giving unto us. Now step forth and mount the altar."

Wick stepped forward.

"Ah-ah," Madame Thatchbore said. "Just her."

Briar sent Wick a look. It was meant to be amused, but Wick could still smell the worry she was trying to stifle. It was not strong, but it was there. He could see her clutch her knife under her loose sleeve, as if to remind herself it was there.

Then Briar shed her robe. It fell to the ground to reveal Briar in all her naked glory, her head held high.

She stepped up to the altar and, after a moment's consideration, began to raise her leg to climb on.

Wick took her hips and lifted. Briar startled, then looked back with a relieved smile as he turned her to face him and placed her onto the altar, her ass resting against the stone.

"We will be fine," Wick assured her.

Briar smiled, amused. "I thought I would be the one reassuring you."

"You are," Wick said. For some reason, comforting her was also comforting him. Focusing on her soft skin and her familiar scent made it easier to bear the weight of all the eyes on him as he shed his loincloth.

Briar's smile grew more solid. She leaned up toward him and whispered, "Wish they could see what's really under there. We'd wake so many women up to wants they didn't even know they had."

Wick had no desire to awaken any woman to her wants except Briar. He stepped between her legs, tugging her to the edge of the altar.

"Let the ritual commence," Madame Thatchbore declared.

A drumbeat rang across the snowy clearing. Wick looked over to see the mud man thudding two sticks slowly against a drum. The man was averting his eyes. He seemed to be the only one; all other eyes were locked on Briar, naked and gorgeous over the smooth stone.

Wick rolled his shoulders, annoyed. He wanted to cover Briar with his body and block them from their expectant gaze.

"There it is," Briar said softly. She ran her fingers up his arm. "Are you getting in your head about it?"

"No," Wick said, tearing his gaze away from the crowd. Still, he could not deny that he was growing soft.

Briar hooked her leg around his waist. "Just focus on me."

Wick nodded. He stepped closer, the front of his thighs pressing against the smooth stone altar. He ignored the crowd, the altar, the candles, and focused instead on Briar in front of him, the amulet lying between her breasts.

We will be fine, he reminded himself.

Briar leaned up and kissed him. The townsfolk melted away, replaced by Briar's lips against his.

Wick kissed her deeply, feeling her groan when she licked her own taste out of his mouth. He could feel her response once more, the thick scent of her slick growing stronger as he rubbed her thighs.

Briar pulled back, her eyes dark. "Get inside me."

She shifted forward, rubbing her entrance against his stiffening cock. Her outer lips parted around Wick's length, and he shuddered.

The drumbeat increased. Wick barely heard it, too busy lining himself up and sinking inside—slowly, shallowly, ever careful to stretch her properly.

Briar made the same shocked noise as always. Her mouth fell open, and Wick ached to push his fingers inside and feel the silk of her tongue.

He resisted. He pulled out of her hole and thrust back inside. Briar had been right to make him stretch her beforehand. He sank in easily until the first ridge popped into her.

Briar keened. "*Wick!*"

Wick bent over her, pressing her into the smooth stone. Keeping her from view. Keeping her from the cold. Wick rocked deeper inside and thought, deliriously, of how much he would like to keep her forever.

The drumbeat hastened once more. The candles swelled, their flames blooming around them as Wick mated her, holding her still against the altar.

Briar's breath came faster, her kisses slack. There was a stage of mating where she could no longer kiss, only breathe excitedly against his mouth. They were reaching it much faster than usual.

Wick sped up, pressing her harder against the stone. The drum beat loudly in his ears, only to be drowned out by his pounding blood.

The amulet glowed, trapped between their bodies.

"Wick," Briar panted, shining with sweat. "Come in me. I want to feel it."

Wick did not think about the frenzy, thrumming wildly just out of reach. He did not think about all the eyes on him. He focused on her, like she told him to, and came so hard his fingers dug into the altar, breaking off crumbs of stone.

The drumbeat stuttered to a halt.

At first, Wick assumed it was because the ritual was over. Then Briar gasped against his cheek, shoving at him.

Wick swayed back. "What is it?"

Briar didn't respond. She stared up at him, her eyes wide with panic.

"Shit," she whispered.

A scream rang over the crowd.

Wick jolted up, his cock sliding out of Briar as he looked at the village folk.

They were clamoring, yelling, and pointing at him in horror. Not at his chest, where the glamor had conjured his head. But his true face, exposed for the whole village to see.

The glamor had failed. They were in the presence of a Skullstalker. Suddenly, the mountain cliff looming overhead was not the biggest terror today.

Briar climbed off the altar, her hands raised. "Everything's okay! He won't hurt you!"

But it was too late. The village was already fleeing, the bowl of gold clattering off the pillar and scattering coins as people ran for the town.

Briar swore. "Wick, time to go!"

Wick turned to her. But before he could wrap her in his arms and take flight, an arrow flew out of the crowd and buried itself in his shoulder.

Wick roared. He whirled to face the shooter, expecting a villager.

A bounty hunter stared back at him. He had wavy

hair and a rakish smile. The last time Wick had seen him, he was outside Wick's cave, telling his gang to retreat.

Renault reloaded his crossbow and aimed a second time, grinning viciously.

"Now," he yelled.

A net descended from the sky and slammed Wick to the ground.

FIFTEEN

Briar wanted to laugh in Renault's stupid, sniggering face.

He really thought he could get his cronies to drop a *net* on Wick? As if some rope could hold him? He was a *Skullstalker*. Naked or not, he could tear that flowery rope apart with one claw.

But Wick smashed into the ground with surprising force. Then his skin started smoking.

Briar yanked her fur robe back on, cursing loudly. Usually when chaos broke loose, it was time to get out of there as fast as possible. But she couldn't leave Wick. Especially not when he was trapped under a flower-knotted net that was burning him.

Briar covered her hands with the fur robe and yanked at the net. Her finger slipped out of the fur onto the thick rope, and she flinched. But her skin didn't blister. Was it only dangerous to Skullstalkers?

Wick's eye cracked open. It was wet and

comfortingly fiery, even if the flames were smaller than she'd ever seen them. He was struggling against the ropes, his movements getting more panicked by the second.

Briar opened her mouth to tell him she would handle it.

"Bri-i-ar," yelled Renault through the fleeing village folk.

Briar bared her teeth and whirled to face him.

Renault strolled calmly through the thinning crowd, stepping around a limping Madame Thatchbore who was staring at Briar while a harried-looking man led her away by the arm.

Renault had two of his cronies at his side. One carried an ax, the other was bending to scoop up the spilled gold from the offering bowl.

"That's mine," Briar snarled.

"Finders keepers." Renault grinned. "Briar, Briar, Briar. I knew the curse would make you desperate. But I never pictured *this*."

He gestured at Wick, who was writhing under the net as it burned through another layer of flesh.

Briar forced her face to stay smooth and unassuming. The knife she had tucked into her long sleeve was tacky with sweat. She let it fall into her hand, still hidden by the fur.

"I'm surprised you manage to capture anybody," she said easily. "They should just run away while you're gloating."

"That's why I have these guys." Renault gestured at

the bounty hunters on either side of him. "They keep everything in place while I'm gloating."

"You just think of everything," Briar said. She squeezed the knife hilt, waiting for him to come close enough to strike. Maybe if she bought Wick enough time, he'd break through the net.

The last of the villagers fled out of sight. They were alone: just Renault, his cronies, Wick, Briar, and the giant ravine next to them.

She nodded at the two hunters on either side of him. "I recognize these two from the village. What happened to the rest?"

"It was a dangerous journey," Renault said. "You'd know. You're the one who talked a Skullstalker into protecting you. Very impressive, Copperwood."

"I'm a very impressive person," Briar said coolly.

Renault's gaze fell to her chest. There was a thin sliver of skin visible where her fur robe was hanging open, shiny with sweat. His eyes darkened.

Briar gripped the knife so hard her fingers ached.

A loud snap echoed through the air.

Briar looked down. Wick had broken one of the ropes, but they were still burning deep into his skin.

"Better speed this up." Renault gestured at his cronies. They advanced on Briar, dragging ropes out of their pockets.

Briar stepped back. She had wanted to catch Renault with the knife first, but it looked like these two would have to go first.

"Careful," Renault said. "Almost going over the ravine."

"How awful that would be for you," Briar replied. "Having to scrape up my carcass for your reward."

She stepped back again, her bare feet teetering on the edge of the ravine.

Renault's smile went sharp and satisfied. "You would never. You don't care about anything more than your life—even spite."

Briar rocked back into place, her heart racing. "I don't know. I like spite an *awful* lot."

The bounty hunter with a bag of gold around his neck lunged for her.

She dodged and shoved him. Renault made an annoyed noise as he disappeared down the ravine, screaming until he hit the ground with a sick *crunch*.

Briar grimaced and looked into the ravine. The man was lying motionless on the rocky bottom; his limbs twisted at hideous angles.

"Alright," Renault muttered. "What am I paying these people for? You, stand back."

The second bounty hunter stood back, looking relieved.

Renault stepped up, his head cocked.

"Now," he said. "Are you going to make this easy or..."

He trailed off.

At first, Briar thought he was staring at her chest again. Then she looked down and saw the amulet glowing.

Another rope snapped. Wick snarled, groping for the next thick strap pinning him down.

"Huh," said Renault. He reached up with his crossbow, sticking the point of the bolt through the amulet chain. "What's this?"

"Nothing," Briar blurted.

Immediately, she knew she had ruined everything. She'd been too desperate, too fast. She closed her sweaty fingers tightly around her knife, the tip peeking out from underneath the fur.

Renault's eyes lit up. "Nothing? Well, then. You won't mind if I do this."

He jerked the crossbow. The chain snapped, and Briar yelled as the amulet went sailing into the ravine.

"Now," Renault repeated. "Are you—?"

A wild roar cut him off. Wick writhed savagely against the bonds, the last rope breaking free against his straining wings.

"Shit," Renault hissed.

Briar reared back and stabbed him in the chest.

Renault stumbled back. Unfortunately, *away* from the ravine. Briar only got to see him stare, stunned, at his bleeding chest before she wrenched the knife out and turned.

Too slow.

The second bounty hunter slammed into her, scrabbling for the knife. But before he could grab it or even get stabbed, his eyes went wide, and he was ripped off of her.

Briar didn't get a chance to enjoy the sight of Wick

tearing into him. She was too busy falling, clutching wildly for any handhold she could find.

Her vision blurred: rocks, blood, the dark cliff looming over the village. Then her fur robe caught on something sharp, and Briar jerked to a stop.

She craned her head. Her robe had snagged on a rock, icy wind curling over her naked legs as she hung there, halfway down the ravine.

Briar cursed. She shoved her knife between her teeth and looked around desperately.

Screams echoed down the ravine. Briar ignored them, cold sweat dripping down her spine as she twisted carefully until she was grabbing the rocks.

Her hands stung against the craggy surface. She gritted her teeth around her blade and started climbing down. Rocks pressed into her bare feet, drawing blood. Briar didn't dare look down or pay attention to the screams overhead. The only thing that existed was the next precarious handhold, the next place to shove her scraped feet.

Finally, she reached the ground. The first bounty hunter lay dead on the rocks, his head cracked open.

The amulet lay several feet away. It was cracked, the glow stuttering before slowly dying.

"Shit," Briar whispered.

She took a step toward it.

The screams stopped.

Briar tensed, waiting for the sound of a crossbow or Renault yelling. Instead, she heard the sound of something whooshing, and Wick roared in feral fury.

Briar looked up just in time to watch him sail over the side of the ravine. He was wrapped in a new net, his naked flesh smoking as he fell.

He hit the ground with a thud that made Briar wince. Despite every instinct yelling at her to run, she turned and took a step toward her gentleman monster.

"Wick?" she whispered. She cleared her throat. "Wick!"

Wick snarled, spittle flying from his jaws. Then, slowly, he quietened.

Briar looked up hopefully. The amulet was glowing faintly on the other side of him.

Wick's head turned. One eye was burned shut. But the other one fixed on her, pained and confused.

"Briar," he croaked. "Did I... Did I hurt...?"

"You didn't hurt me," Briar said, her voice choked with useless tears. "I'm okay, everything's fine."

She ran toward him.

Wick spasmed, a horrifying noise ripping out of his throat. "STOP!"

Briar stopped, clutching her fur robe. "What?"

Wick writhed. In pain or against the blood frenzy, she wasn't sure.

"It is not working," he managed. "You have to... hurt me."

"Void take you," Briar said with a terrified laugh. "I don't have to do anything. You just need the amulet. It's right over there!"

She took another step toward it.

Wick screamed, the noise turning thick and feral halfway through. He jerked against his bonds, snapping a rope over his leg.

"I cannot hold myself back," he cried, agonized. "You must, you *must*. Before I break free. I can feel it burning inside—"

He cut off. His cry was so pained that Briar flinched with him.

"Please," he whispered.

That fiery eye fixed on hers. Then the flame shivered and blew into a wildfire, burning so huge it took over the black.

Briar stumbled to the other side of the ravine, facing away from the town. Their flowers were clustered at the top, rustling merrily in the cold breeze.

Briar stared up at the steep rocks. There were enough handholds to get down, which meant there were enough to get back up. If she just had enough time—

Wick screamed. It was not a pained scream. It was *hungry*.

Another rope snapped on his net.

"Fuck," Briar burst, her voice cracking. She didn't have enough time. If she started climbing, he would just fly after her. Unless...

Briar turned back toward him, numb.

She had done so many loathsome things in her life that she had lost count. But walking toward Wick felt like the worst.

Wick twisted and snapped as she approached. But he

was pinned to the rock, helpless to do anything but roar and twist as she walked up behind him and pressed her blade to the base of his left wing.

Sixteen

Wick woke up in more pain than he had ever known.

One of his eyes would only open halfway. It felt strange and swollen, throbbing with the same unbearable heat as so much of his body.

He groaned, struggling to sit up. He had an arrow in his shoulder, and the last shards of net twisted around his horns. Burns coated his body, thick stripes sinking into the bone.

It was dark. He was lying at the bottom of a ravine. Dim memories ran through his mind: the bounty hunter Renault, stinking of lipseed as he shot an arrow into Wick's shoulder. A net of Malblosom, making him blister. Mortal skin opening under his claws. A neck parting under his fangs. Telling a bloodied Briar to run while tears dripped down her cheeks. She was with him here, at the bottom of the ravine.

He could not remember watching her escape.

He *did* remember a voice. That cold, rocky voice that had snuck in during Marigold's spell. Under the blood frenzy, the voice was a whisper no longer. This had been a low hiss that swelled into a scream, telling him to fight, telling him to *kill*.

He forced the memory away, focusing instead on the memory of Briar's terrified face.

"Briar," he rasped.

He looked around. A savaged mortal body made his slow heartbeat stutter, but upon closer inspection, it was not Briar. It was one of the bounty hunters who had foolishly engaged them.

He looked up.

The town side of the ravine was naked and rocky. The forbidden side of the ravine—the side none of them were allowed to cross—was covered in vines, leading up to a thicket of flowers.

But the vines ended abruptly above Wick's head. They had been torn out, the rock underneath them savaged with claw marks. Wick must have tried to climb out, then slid back down to the bottom of the ravine.

Wick blinked blearily. *Why did I not just fly?*

He attempted to stretch his wings. A bolt of agony ran through him, making him roar.

He groped behind him. Another jagged bolt of pain confirmed what his fingers told him: his left wing was gone.

A tremulous voice came from the top of the ravine. "Wick?"

Wick craned his head.

Briar's tearful face poked out from the top of the ravine. She saw him and made a soft, wounded noise.

"Gods, you look..." She swallowed hard. "Are you okay?"

"I am fine," Wick replied instantly. "Are *you* okay? Did I hurt you?"

Briar laughed wetly. "I'm great! *You* didn't hurt *me*."

The intention behind her words was obvious. Her voice was heavy with guilt, tears dripping down her chin. She was wearing the fur coat she had been wearing before the ritual, her borrowed clothes underneath it. She had her pack strapped to her back, her fingers white around the straps.

Wick flexed his wings, or more accurately, one wing and one torn stub. It sent another stab of agony through him. His flightless existence stretched before him, strange and daunting. But it was worth it if it made Briar safe.

Briar sniffed. "You can climb up. The stone is brittle, don't dig your claws in too far."

Wick looked up at the claw marks he had gouged into the cliff. He had been too feral to realize he should have changed his climbing technique. He had never been grateful to be completely feral. If he had any intelligence left, he would have climbed the ravine properly, and Briar would be dead.

"Wait," Briar called as he hooked his claws carefully into the rock. "The amulet is down there with you!"

Wick stopped and looked around. The amulet was lying near the dead bounty hunter, its chain broken and the metal cracked.

"No," Wick whispered.

He picked up the amulet and rubbed it hopefully. It flickered, white light spasming into his palm before dying a swift death.

Wick picked up his loincloth next, which was tangled on a rock nearby. "Perhaps I should stay down here."

"To the void with *that*," Briar said harshly. "Get up here right now or I'll climb down!"

"Do *not*," Wick growled. There was nowhere to run in this ravine. At least she would have a chance on the forbidden side of the ravine.

He jerked the arrow out of his shoulder and licked the wound carefully. He still hadn't fully recovered from the last arrow wound on his other shoulder.

He tied his loincloth around his waist, careful against the painful burns. "Has the village bothered you?"

"They haven't been back." Briar wiped her cheeks and stared across the ravine, presumably at the stone altar. "I thought I saw Renault earlier. But I can't be sure."

Wick braced himself against the cliff. "Did he smell of lipseed?"

Briar stared at him. "What? I—I suppose he would, he uses it in his hair. But I wasn't close enough to get a sniff."

Wick nodded. He had temporarily forgotten that mortal noses were so weak.

He began to climb, the amulet tucked into his palm. Every small movement made his burned skin scream. He gritted his fangs and forced himself to reach for the next rock, digging his claws in as hard as he dared.

But not too hard. He had control. In this moment, anyhow, he was himself again.

Briar watched him climb, her eyes still wet. She clutched the side of the ravine, crushing several of the flowers they had been sent to collect.

"You have found the flowers," Wick said, attempting to make her smile.

Briar did. It was small and tremulous, but she smiled enough that, for a moment, Wick barely noticed his injuries. Then he lifted his arm to haul himself up further, and every agony came wailing back with an intensity that made him lock up against the wall.

"Wick?" Briar shifted like she was going to reach for him.

"I am fine," Wick called. "Stay there."

Briar sat back, frowning. Her face and hands were covered in tiny marks that made Wick imagine her making this very same climb, her fragile human skin giving way so easily to the unforgiving rocks.

He neared the top of the ravine. Briar started pulling at his arm to help him the rest of the way, a move so useless and sweet that Wick huffed a pained laugh and let her continue.

He heaved himself over the top of the ravine and braced himself against the ground, panting.

"Shit," Briar whispered. She tugged the remaining shards of net off his horns, throwing them away. "Wick. *Gods.*"

Wick held out the amulet. "Take it."

Briar took it. It gleamed stronger than before, but Briar barely looked at it before stuffing it into her fur coat.

"Hey, look at me." She cupped his face carefully, avoiding the burns. "It's not actually that bad! I think your eye is already better; it was all the way shut yesterday."

"Yesterday," Wick repeated. He looked up at the dark sky. He had assumed it had only been a few hours. But a day?

He looked down at Briar and inhaled. There was pain in her scent, mixing with the worry.

"Your curse is taking hold," he said. "You are hurting."

"*I'm* hurting?" Briar barked a laugh so loud and harsh that it truly did sound like a bark, a snarling animal noise deep in her throat.

She smacked him in the arm. "You are *impossible*, you know that? Huh, gentleman monster? You're just—"

She gnashed her teeth and turned, blinking hard. When she looked back at him, her eyes were very nearly dry.

"Come on," she said. "I found a cave."

Tucked safely out of sight was a tall, thin cave. Wick barely had to duck when Briar led him into it. He did not even have to pull his wings in, although that was most likely because he only had one now. It scraped the stone as he shuffled inside.

It should have hurt. But he was in so much pain he barely felt it—deep burns and the blunt loss of his wing, which ached deeper than a wound. He would never fly again. He had not known how much he enjoyed flying before it was gone.

Briar came to a stop in front of a strange, tangled lump. Unfamiliar items of clothing lay in a misshapen pile: coats and shirts and other items of clothing that Wick did not know the name of, soft and billowy.

"Here," Briar said. "This is yours."

It took Wick a moment to realize what he was looking at.

"You made me a nest," he realized.

Briar shrugged and sat down next to the nest. She hauled her pack into her lap and cradled it like he had once seen a mortal child hold a stuffed toy.

"Best I could do," she said, muffled into the pack. "I stole people's shit when I snuck back into the village for supplies. Got you food, too."

She nodded at the back of the cave. A dead rabbit was lying on a rock, already skinned. The fur had been added to the nest, Wick noted with surprise. It was lying on the top, as Wick did with his own nest.

He stroked the rabbit fur. Then he sat down, ignoring the pain from his burns as they came into contact with the nest. It was admittedly very soft, even if it was structurally useless. Everything squashed out underneath him as soon as he lowered himself. And yet,

Wick was almost content. If he were not in such pain, it might have been a deeply lovely night.

"This is the nicest thing any creature has ever done for me," Wick told her.

Briar stared at him, her bright eyes gleaming. For a moment, Wick feared she would burst into tears.

"Fuck you," she said instead.

Wick blinked. "What?"

"Nothing." Briar's mouth twisted horribly, and she buried her face in her hands. "You're *so... ugh!* And it's all the time! Every day! Every void-damned second, and now you're hurt, I hurt you, and you're *still like this*!"

The last words were a wail into her hands. Wick's tail flicked uncertainly. The movement jarred several burns. He stilled.

"I do not understand why you're angry at me," he said honestly. "But it must wait. Your curse is burning hotter."

He sniffed the air. The fire was encroaching on her heart, fierce and unyielding.

He took her wrist and pulled her into his lap, watching her eyes widen.

"You want to do this now? You're covered in burns!"

"I will survive," he assured her. "You would not."

She readjusted herself on his lap. She was holding herself strangely, like she wanted to place the least amount of pressure on him as possible.

"If you are afraid of the blood frenzy," he tried. "I will take you back to the town."

Briar rolled her eyes. She took the amulet out of her pocket, eyed the crack down the middle, and then tied a knot in the chain.

"I'd rather risk you," she said as she slid the knotted necklace around her throat. "I just... I don't want to hurt you."

Her face crumpled.

"I *really* hurt you," she whispered.

Wick was made of pain. Briar's weight on him should have made it worse, and in some ways it did. But in other ways, ways that went deeper than these scorch marks, her weight on him was the only thing keeping him from falling into agony.

"I told you to," Wick said. "I am glad you did it."

"Oh, he's *glad*." Briar's face twisted once more. "I can't *believe*—"

Wick shushed her, pressing a scarred finger to her lip. Then he bent down and kissed her as gently as he was able. He suddenly wanted nothing more than to bury himself in her and forget this day had happened.

Briar kissed back desperately. She flung her arms around his shoulders, her touch both forceful and hesitant as she attempted to lie them only on places where he was unburned.

"What in the void *was* that net made out of?" she asked when she paused to take her pants off, leaving her shirt intact. "It didn't burn me."

"Malblossom," he replied. "Please talk of something else."

Briar nodded fervently and stroked his chest. She was looking at him with an intensity that he recognized: she did not want to think about it, either. She did not want the memories, which she had to keep in full, whereas he only had glimpses washed in crimson. She wanted to forget herself in him, just as he did.

She did not undo his loincloth completely. She only lowered it, letting it pillow around his thighs to cushion her weight. Even with all the pain, he was already half-hard when she pulled his cock free.

"Thank the gods *this* isn't burned," she said.

Wick made a noise of agreement and watched her brace herself over his hardening cock.

"Do you want—" Wick paused to receive a hard kiss. "Do you want my tongue?"

Briar shook her head. "I can take it."

She pushed her fingers inside herself until she was wet. His own come slid out of her, and Wick growled despite himself at the memory of taking her over the altar.

"Don't move," she said breathlessly.

Wick nodded. He gripped her hips, only easing up when his burned hands twinged.

Briar guided his cockhead to her entrance and sank down. It took several attempts for her to work the head inside, making Wick think back to that very first time, back in his own cave. She had been so guarded, even when she began to go lax with pleasure. Now, barely a week later, she was staring up at him as if he had cracked her open and could see everything inside.

She was so beautiful. Bruised and desperate and overwhelmed, but so beautiful she took his breath away, even now.

"You are magnificent," he told her as she rode him, unable to keep silent. "You are so lovely. You feel—"

She made a lost noise and kissed him again. The hard edge of the skull mask dug into her cheek, and Wick wondered if it pained her. If it did, she made no recognition of it, her kisses getting more and more forceful as she rode him.

The first ridge slid inside. Briar moaned against his mouth.

Wick reached down to touch her clit.

She knocked his hand away. "I said, don't move. Just... let me..."

She trailed off, mouth opening on a cry. She rode him faster. She could not take him very deep, but she was squeezing around him so tightly that Wick could feel his orgasm coming up fast. And with it, the blood frenzy.

He watched the amulet hanging lopsidedly under her shirt. The blood frenzy was pulsing at the edges of his mind, gaining territory—

Then the amulet glowed, flickering and faulty, but enough to drive the blood frenzy out.

They both sighed in relief. Briar rode faster, her hips faltering as he twitched inside her.

Wick waited for her to say something that would tip him over the edge, as she often did. But Briar just panted, her face twisting as she thickened the air with so many emotions that he could not tell them apart. She was frustrated, and he could tell she wanted him to turn her over and take her properly. But she also seemed to be chasing something larger than release, stroking his skull mask as she mated him.

"Wick," she whimpered. "*Wick.*"

Wick squeezed her hips still and came with a muffled grunt. The orgasm washed over him in waves, drowning out the pain. He held her in place, as they both looked down to watch his cock pulse come into her.

Briar's eyelids fluttered. Her mouth opened on a hazy moan as come dripped out of her hole and down Wick's cock, pooling on his balls.

Briar's hips jolted, drawing out one last pulse of come that made them both moan.

"I missed this," Briar panted. "I thought— I thought I would never get it again."

Wick stroked her hair. He was growing soft, but Briar gripped him so he did not slip out.

"Stay," she said quietly. "Stay inside me. I want to feel it."

Wick thought she meant to keep it inside for the duration of her own release. But she guided him on top of her until he was pressing her into the nest. Then she clung to him, her breathing slowing until she fell asleep.

Wick waited until the smell of sleep was thick. Then he slipped out of her with a wet noise, ignoring how much he wanted to stuff her with his now half-hard cock until he came again. Then he leaned out of the nest and groped for her pack until he found her knife.

He placed it in her hands. Then he lay down beside her, nuzzling as close as he dared.

A knife would not do much if it came to it. But it was better than nothing.

SEVENTEEN

Briar had never been a caretaker before.

She always thought that if she got roped into it, she would do a purposefully lackluster job. But she found herself putting all of herself into taking care of Wick as he healed in their tiny cave behind the Yedzeva ravine, catching him rabbits to eat. Fluffing up his nest with new stolen clothing. Polishing his horns. Bandaging his wounds. Taking quick breaks to rub herself clean with snow, rushing back into the cave as fast as she could, not only because she was freezing, but in case he needed her. Gathering herbal creams from the village to soothe his burns, rubbing them on him every morning and night. Wick insisted they were helping, but he also said Skullstalkers healed much faster than humans, so Briar couldn't tell if his rapid healing was because of her or not.

"There's no other way out," she told him as she rubbed oil into his horns. There was nothing medical about it, she just saw some oil when she was sneaking around the village and decided to treat him.

"I'll sneak us out at night," she continued. "No problem."

Wick raised his head to give her an amused look. He had spent the last few days in the shoddy nest Briar had built him, insisting that it was truly the best thing anyone had ever done for him, even though there were times on that first day when he was practically sitting on the ground.

"*You* will sneak us out," he repeated, lowering his head again so Briar could resume her work on his horns. "Where will I be? Hiding in your pack?"

"You know what I mean." Briar rubbed an easy circle around his horns, careful of a burn creeping up near the right base.

"I'll *guide* us out," she corrected. "You know how many times I've had to stealth my way out of someplace? And I'll do it again. Nobody will see us. Not the towns-folk, and not..."

She trailed off. Wick picked up on it, like always.

"You said he was gravely injured," he said.

Briar shrugged. Renault *had* been gravely injured, and she wished he'd injured him more. The lipseed-stinking bastard.

"So were you," she said. "And you're fine."

"I heal quickly," Wick said. "Even from Malblossom."

Briar snorted, rubbing his horns harder. She had been going over those flowers in her head, mapping them out until she could recognize them on sight. She had even crept back to the ravine and examined the net. She had seen something like it before, but only in passing. She never paid much attention to monster hunters. According to Wick, many of them didn't even carry Malblossom nets. There were not many rules for fighting Skullstalkers, except to pray to whatever god you believe in and hope your death is swift.

"My eye is already back to normal," Wick continued.

Briar tilted his head up to check. Wick's eye *was* back to normal, not counting some discoloration at the edge.

She stood back, holding her shiny hands at her sides as she examined the burns peeking out from the bandages. The burns were no longer black or angry red, but a vivid pink. On a mortal, it would be unheard of. She had never been so happy that he was a Skullstalker.

"And the rest of you?" she asked. "How's the pain?"

"I am fine." Wick smiled. "Itchy. But fine."

She smiled back. Of course she did. She always did, even when it took everything she had in her not to burst into tears. Every time she looked at him, her eyes were drawn to the lone wing at his back. Even if he was facing her, it was unmistakable what she'd done to him.

She couldn't get past it. She took his *limb*. He should be cursing her, swearing revenge.

"Briar," Wick said. "I said I am *fine*."

Briar breathed out hard through her nose. Then she smiled harder, forcing any uncomfortable emotion underneath it.

"I know what would make you feel even better," she said.

She pressed her oil-slick hand to his belly, avoiding the bandages. They both watched it slide down, reaching under his loincloth and closing around his length.

Wick's eyes drifted shut. The tension in his face drained away, and Briar felt something in her own chest loosen.

It was not easy, fucking when Wick was injured like this. But it was the only time Briar had felt okay since she cut off Wick's wing.

Seven days after the ravine, they finally made it back to the mountain path.

"Told you we wouldn't get caught," Briar whispered.

Wick grunted. He had been shockingly quiet as they crept through the dark village of Yedzeva. Hadn't bumped into anything. He had even stopped Briar before she stepped into a noisy child's toy—one of the many advantages to being able to see in the dark.

Briar waited until they were further down the path before dropping back to her usual volume. "Are you sure you don't need to rest? Give us an hour, and we should be safe to camp."

"I can keep going," Wick said.

Briar eyed his wounds. They had run out of bandages the night before, so the burns stood out clearly on his skin. They were calming down much faster than they would on a mortal, and his most recent arrow wound was already growing new skin. And his wing...

Briar cleared her throat. "We'll see how you feel in an hour. Do you want any more rabbit?"

Wick gave her an amused look that Briar took to mean, *I barely need to eat once a month, mortal. Stop offering me food.*

"Just being polite," Briar muttered. She took a strip of cooked rabbit meat out of her pocket and bit into it.

The moonlight was brighter up ahead. The further Briar walked, the more she realized that it wasn't a trick of the light: the moonlight cut off in a sharp line.

She looked up. The cliff looming over Yedzeva stopped directly above them.

"Still standing," Wick said.

Briar nodded. "Guess the ritual worked. The mountain's wrath won't strike them down this year."

She meant it as a joke. But Wick stayed there, staring up at the cliff with that same strange look he had adopted several times when they talked about the mountain.

Briar shifted nervously. She wanted to get away from the village. She wanted to get back to Marigold and hand over the flower. She wanted their curses gone so she could stop worrying Wick was going to go feral and rip her throat out every time they had sex; there had been some close calls, the amulet flickering so hard she worried it would fail like it had in the ravine.

She cleared her throat.

"Any voices?" she asked, dreading the answer.

Wick shook his head. After one last lingering look, he

turned back to the path and continued walking, only a small limp in his step.

It was light outside when they finally set up camp on a mountain edge.

Briar yawned, staring out at the land below. If she squinted, she could almost see Marigold's cottage through the distant trees.

She pointed. "How long do you think it's going to take us to get down there?"

Wick gave her a long look that she eventually translated as, *Any long distance I've ever traveled, I have flown there. I have no reference for long-distance travel on foot.*

"Right," Briar muttered, ignoring a stab of guilt. "Never mind. I'll set us up a nest."

"You do not have to," Wick said. "I have slept on the ground many times. You have watched me."

"Yes, but still." Briar took the pack Wick had been carrying and dumped the stolen clothes out on the ground and piled them into the best nest she could construct. It still looked awful.

Wick sat down in the middle and held out an expectant hand. "Do you want to mate first? It is another day."

"Charmer," Briar said. But despite her tiredness and her sore hole, she wouldn't say no to a nice fuck right now. She deserved some reward for all that walking.

She took off her pants and started to climb on top of him. But Wick caught her waist and lowered her into the badly made nest.

"I will take you with my tongue first," he said firmly.

Briar let out a surprised laugh. "If you say so."

Wick nodded. But Briar could see how slow every movement was, how careful he had to be with anything that might pull his shoulders, where the deepest burns were.

Briar closed her eyes, forcing herself to focus on how his huge hands dipped underneath her shirt to explore her breasts.

"You just want to fuck me deeper," she said breathily. "The more you stretch me, the more ridges you can fit inside."

Wick made a noise against her belly. He would not take her shirt off—she hadn't throughout the last few days, except to take a freezing snow bath—but he did push up the fabric, kissing and nipping at her skin.

"That is part of it," he admitted. "But mostly I just missed how you taste."

With that, he moved down and pushed her legs apart. He rubbed her skin, something he had started doing when he noticed her shivering on the second day. His hands were some of the least burned parts of his body, but she could feel the puckered edge of a burn on a few fingers.

If it pained him, he showed no sign of it. He nuzzled her thigh and pressed his tongue to the sweat gathering there.

"I missed how you squeeze around my tongue," he continued. "There is nothing like it. I do not often hunger for food, but I hunger for this."

Briar wanted to make a joke about how she shouldn't have hunted for so many rabbits over the past few days. But then Wick's tongue ran over her folds, and the words trailed off into a moan.

After, Wick bundled her in that fur robe and held her close.

"Did I hurt you?" he asked, as he often did.

Briar propped her chin on his chest and smiled. "Only the good kind, big boy."

He frowned. "I still do not understand what you mean."

Briar rubbed her eyes. It was hard to think after she'd just had her brains fucked out like she'd been wanting for days. She liked riding Wick, but there was nothing quite like being held down and fucked.

And she *did* like the inevitable pain that came with fucking a Skullstalker—the impossible stretching, the pressure, fangs nicking her lip and claws pressing into her skin. But more than that, she liked that he wanted to make sure she liked it. Call her a soft touch, but she enjoyed it when men preferred not to hurt her, even if she wanted them to.

"Like when I bite your lip," she explained. "It's painful, but it's nice. As long as it's something you want, it's good."

Wick grunted. His tail wrapped around her leg distractedly. "You will tell me if it is too much?"

"I always do," Briar soothed.

Wick nodded and shifted carefully onto his side, keeping her tucked against him. "Sleep well, my sweet thief."

The nickname made something dangerously soft curl in her chest.

"Back at you, big boy," she whispered.

She pulled the fur robe tighter around her, wishing she could feel Wick's arms more. But he was cold, and they were on a mountain, which meant she was stuck tucking something warm between them while she slept.

Wick shifted and grunted in pain.

Briar was suddenly wide awake. "What is it? Let me see."

"I am fine," he insisted. "Sleep."

She narrowed her eyes at him. "Tell me what it is, and I'll sleep."

Wick sighed, a sound she was sure he had picked up from her. "It *is* nothing. I simply put pressure on my wings."

Wing, Briar corrected silently, her stomach twisting into guilty knots.

She sat up. "Let me look at it. I should have stopped to steal more bandages when I was in that village. Void take them. They owe us *much* more than bandages."

"Briar," Wick consoled.

Briar shushed him and crawled around the nest until she could see his back. It was mostly unscarred; his wings had protected him from most of the net.

The wing stub looked better than yesterday. Skin was already growing over the bone, shiny and pink. Whatever had hurt Wick, it wasn't anything that Briar needed to check.

But Briar didn't move away.

She reached out, not daring to touch. She still hadn't touched the stub, even when she was treating the rest of his wounds. She couldn't bear to see what she'd done.

"Do…" Briar swallowed. "Do Skullstalker wings grow back?"

Wick's silence was answer enough.

Briar laughed. What else could she do? She had been asking as a joke, mostly. But the reality of it struck her again, making her eyes burn and her throat close up.

"I'm sorry," she said, still trying to smile. "I'm—Gods, Wick, I can't tell you how fucking sorry I am."

Wick twisted, tugging her carefully into his arms despite her protests.

"I would tell you to cut off the other wing if it meant saving you," he said.

Briar couldn't look at him. His eyes were so earnest, even huge and black and full of fire. They were the loveliest eyes she'd ever seen. She had no idea how she had grown so attached to them like this.

"Why?" she burst out, wiping angrily at her cheeks. "I'm—I'm just—"

A thief, she thought. *A liar. A trickster with a blackened heart and open legs.*

"I'm just a mortal," she said instead. "You'll live the rest of your impossibly long life not being able to fly because of *me*."

He took her face in her hands, his claws gentle as he

rubbed her cheeks. "Your two hundred years are worth more than thousands of mine."

"Don't say that," Briar snapped. Then his words sank in. "Wait, two hundred? We live for eighty years, *maybe*."

Wick blinked. The fire in his eyes flickered with surprise.

"Eighty?"

"Less, for someone like me!" Briar grinned mirthlessly. "Thieves don't have high life expectancies. I'm shocked I made it this far."

Wick's hands tightened on her face. His mouth worked wordlessly, struggling against something important. Then he steeled himself.

"I would find a way," he said. "There are spells, ancient and difficult, but they are there. I have a brother who can show us how to extend your life. If you wish."

Briar's mouth fell open, shocked. Was he really offering what she thought he was offering?

"You want..." Briar wet her lips, dazed. "You want a *life*? With me?"

Wick nodded eagerly.

Briar let out a disbelieving laugh. Her eyes were filling with tears once more, and she couldn't stop it.

For a moment, Briar let herself imagine nights with him—more than they had lined up on their journey. A lifetime of nights huddled up in his arms, listening to his slow heartbeat. He would be a cool balm in the summer, and a blanket tucked between them during the winter. They could buy a place near a waterfall—

Briar squeezed her eyes shut, forcing the ideas to

stop. She couldn't think about this right now. Not without bursting into tears and becoming utterly useless.

They would break their respective curses. Then... Briar would think about it.

"We should sleep," she said, lying back down in the nest. "Lots of walking tomorrow."

Wick said nothing. But his big arms closed around her, making sure her robe was tight around her body before settling in for the night.

Eighteen

Wick had never been more relieved to hear a waterfall.

He stopped, his head cocked.

Briar stopped with him, looking up at him expectantly. "What is it?"

"We are close," he replied.

Briar let out a heavy breath, her shoulders sagging with relief. "*Finally*. I need to eat a vegetable that isn't those awful turnip things we found yesterday. I hope Marigold has something cooking."

Wick sniffed the air. There was only the scent of trees, water, and the weariness and worry that had been clinging to Briar for days. The scent of his own injuries had faded into the background much easier than Briar's anxiety.

"I do not smell anything," he said. "But we can hope."

Briar smiled. It was stronger than many of the smiles

she had given him since the ravine, although she averted her eyes very quickly. She seemed to have trouble looking directly at him since yesterday, when he offered to extend her life so she could spend it with him.

Wick wondered if he'd overstepped. But he was used to his overstepping with mortals ending in screaming and bloodshed. If this was Briar's reaction, he could cope with that.

They continued through the trees until they came across the waterfall. It was bubbling merrily, and Wick gave it a longing glance before turning toward the cottage.

Marigold was facing away from them, spinning her staff distractedly. She was staring up at the trees. Wick almost assumed she was looking for them, but that would not make sense. They were coming from the opposite direction.

Briar dug into her pack and came out with a handful of the flowers they had been sent to collect.

"We're back," she called. "Fashionably late. Hope you didn't miss us."

Marigold jumped, her staff jolting out of her hands.

"Gods," she gasped. She stared at them, open-mouthed, looking at her staff and then at Briar before seemingly deciding that her discarded staff could wait.

She ran up to Briar and flung herself into Briar's arms, squeezing her tightly. "What *happened*? I expected you back a week ago; the glamor can't last that long. You were supposed to fly right—"

She stammered to a stop, staring up at Wick, covered

in healing burns. She pointed at his remaining wing. "You used to have two of those."

"I did," Wick agreed.

"Hence why we're back so late." Briar smiled in a way that reminded Wick of wolves baring their teeth. "Here's your flower. Hope it was worth the trouble."

She held out the flowers she had been carrying carefully in her pack for days.

Marigold stared at it. Then she jumped, grabbing it like she had only remembered why she was excited about it.

"Right," she said, flustered. "Good! I'm just sorry it was so much trouble. What happened up there?"

"We had a charming interaction with the locals," Briar drawled. She looked up at Wick and continued, "Remember when we thought the sex ritual would be the most notable part about our trip?"

"Sex ritual? Ha!" Marigold let out a screechy laugh, bending down to scoop up her staff. Then she noticed that Briar was not joking. "Oh. Wow. You're serious? I really did hope those were just rumors."

"I'll tell you the story over food," Briar said. "What do you have in your kitchen?"

She linked arms with Marigold, the two of them heading toward the house. Wick moved to follow, then froze as he caught a faint whiff of something familiar on Marigold's skin.

Briar noticed him stop and turned to him, her arm loosening around Marigold's. "Wick? What is it?"

Wick wanted to tell her. But now was not the time.

Not with Marigold standing right there, gripping her staff unexpectedly tight.

"I will stay out here and wash," Wick told them.

Briar frowned. "Do you need help?"

"I will be fine," Wick said, unable to keep his fondness or his nerves from creeping into his tone.

Marigold laughed. "Since when do you help Skullstalkers *wash*? Does he need someone to scrub his back?"

Briar's frown hardened. Marigold's laugh died a swift death as she looked back at Wick's injuries and made the connection.

"Oh," Marigold said. "I'm sorry. I'm sure Briar can—"

"I will be fine," Wick repeated, firmer this time. "I will see you after you finish eating."

Briar's eyes narrowed. She was onto him, he was sure of it. But she pulled up a smile that got so close to carefree it almost fooled him and tugged Marigold toward the cottage once more.

"I hope you have biscuits," Wick heard her say.

He watched them vanish into the house. He did not move toward the waterfall, even though he would badly like to bathe. He breathed in, the scent still lingering in the air where Marigold had been standing.

Lipseed. Just a faint whiff of it, but enough to make Wick pause. It was not common in this region, nor anywhere he had traveled with Briar. In this part of the country, he only ever smelled it on rich mortals' hair or skin, rubbed there with oils.

Suspicion churned in Wick's gut. He hoped he was wrong.

But he doubted it.

Not long later, Briar came to meet him at the waterfall.

"You were taking too long," she announced as she pulled her clothes off and left them in a pile on the grassy bank. She climbed into the water and stretched, satisfied.

"*So* nice to get naked and not have my nipples immediately turn to icicles," she told him.

Wick smiled reflexively. He had been doing it more since Briar showed up. He always considered it a mortal gesture, one he avoided. Skullstalkers saw the act of showing their teeth as a threat, after all. But he could not stop himself from smiling as Briar waded up to him, her eyes roving over him in a way she would forever deny was concerned.

"I can bathe myself," Wick told her gently.

"What? I know. This is purely selfish." Briar's gaze turned heated, her smile curling in anticipation as she placed a hand on his chest. "I'm using you for my pleasure."

"And making sure you do not die," Wick reminded her.

"And that. Whatever." Briar tilted her face up, her eyes going half-lidded as she watched his mouth.

Wick swayed toward her, unable to stop himself. For a moment, all he wanted in the world was those soft lips on his, her warm body pressed against him. She was more relaxed than she had been in days. She was already wet, her sweet smell drifting up and making his mouth water and cock harden.

Wick stopped her just before their lips touched. "Your witch. Does she ever use lipseed in her spells?"

Briar blinked, surprised. "Don't see why she would. I'm no expert, but that stuff is pretty useless for spells. Food, too. You only use it to pretty yourself up. Why?"

That was what Wick had been fearing.

He stepped back, letting Briar's hand fall from his belly. "Your witch smells of it. Not enough for a mortal to notice."

Briar laughed disbelievingly. "You think she... what? She arranged for Renault and his merry gang of bounty hunters to meet us in that village?"

"I do not know," Wick said, but Briar was already talking over him.

"You think, what, he just swanned up here with a knife, and she immediately caved? She would have told me if she was being threatened. We have a secret code to tip each other off!"

"I don't," Wick tried.

Briar continued, her scent full of fury, "Or do you think he showed her a bag of money, and she immediately jumped on board?"

"Briar," Wick said.

"*Don't*," she snapped. She shoved a finger in his face, her teeth bared in a way that made him think of Skullstalker rules: a smile was a threat. "You think my oldest friend—my *only* friend—is fucking me over?"

Wick frowned. "I thought I was your friend."

Briar hesitated. For a second, he thought she would stop hissing at him and have a conversation. Then her expression closed off, her scent getting duller in the way it always did when she was forcing herself not to feel something.

She turned and stormed back to the riverbank.

"Briar," Wick repeated. "Your curse."

"It's not even dark yet," Briar spat as she pulled her clothes over her damp legs. "Stay there. I'm just— I'm gonna—"

She looked back at the cottage, her face hardening.

"You're wrong," she told him. "I'll prove it."

"It's not safe," Wick argued.

Briar shot him an angry look. "It's *Marigold*! I'm safe with her. If I'm safe with *anyone*, I'm safe with her. Stay there."

She marched off. Wick watched her go, every part of him wanting to follow. He had only gone to the waterfall because he knew he would hear Briar if she was in trouble.

He took a step toward the bank.

A voice in his mind stopped him, cold and rocky. It was the voice that had been haunting him and several other Skullstalkers for their whole lives. It was brief, barely lasting a heartbeat. But it was surprisingly loud, like it was on the mountain, loud enough to make him stumble against the river rocks.

Soon, it whispered.

Nineteen

Briar marched into the cottage, her mind reeling.

It couldn't be true, she told herself as she headed through the cluttered rooms. It had to be a mistake. Maybe Marigold was finally trying something other than Forest Girl Fashion, which she wore even as a street urchin. Maybe she *did* use the oil for spells. There *had* to be a reason Wick smelled it on her that didn't have anything to do with her brutally betraying her oldest friend.

Briar came to a stop in the hallway, heart pounding. She could hear Marigold in the kitchen, humming and occasionally swearing as she puttered about.

Briar could go in and confront her. Get this mess smoothed out. But there was a suspicion itching in the back of her head. Why did Wick hear that strange, cold voice when Marigold was inside his head? How could Renault have *possibly* known they would be in Yedzeva? And Marigold seemed even more scatterbrained than usual. Oddly strained. Briar had chalked it down to hosting a Skullstalker, but what if it was more than that?

Briar gritted her teeth. She always told herself that if she could trust anyone, it was Marigold. Was she really about to let some Skullstalker—a *monster*—make her doubt that, just because they had been journeying together for a few weeks?

Marigold's humming grew louder. It was a tune they had made up together in the orphanage, just before Marigold left to be trained as a witch.

Briar looked toward the kitchen. Then she turned away and headed toward Marigold's bedroom.

The door was sealed. Magically, so Briar couldn't even pick the lock.

Luckily, she knew Marigold well enough to know she would have forgotten a key insight: thieves also climbed through windows.

Briar snuck around the cottage and climbed through the window, landing softly on her damp feet. She grimaced at the footprints—she would have to erase those before she left—and then looked around the messy room.

Marigold was many things, but a criminal mastermind was not one of them. Even when they were on the streets and scouring for food after the orphanage ran out, she left it up to Briar to come up with plans. *And* to save them when the plan inevitably went awry. If she locked the door, she would assume that she didn't need to hide many of her secrets. That was just the sort of life she had led.

Briar looked through the nightstand. Then the dresser. Then her desk, strewn with notes spilling over from her study, orders from clients, and half-finished letters. An ornate hairpin that she had let Marigold borrow and then never gotten back.

She was reaching for the hairpin when a certain envelope caught her eye.

It was freshly sliced open. The seal was ordinary, no crest to give it away. But she recognized the handwriting in the letter that had been pulled out of it.

Heart sinking, Briar picked it up.

I am glad we have come to an understanding, the letter said in Renault's stupid, swoopy handwriting. *You will receive your money as soon as the Briar girl is secured.*

Footsteps echoed down the hall. Heavy, because Marigold never had to live in the shadows like she had. She'd spent most of her life cozy and warm, her belly full. And she had *still* sold Briar out.

Briar had just enough time to drop the envelope and pick up the hairpin, not bothering to turn around. Only guilty people did that.

After the smallest flash of light, the door swung open.

Marigold spluttered. "Briar! What are you doing in here?"

"Getting my hairpin back." Briar turned slowly, lazily, as if nothing was wrong. It was important not to panic in these situations. Even if everything in her wanted to grab Marigold, shake her until her eyes bled, and demand to know how much coin it took to betray her.

Marigold's empty hands flexed at her sides. She was wishing she'd kept her staff with her, Briar realized. She was worried Briar had found out.

"You could have asked me to let you in," Marigold said with a nervous titter. "Did you come in through the window?"

"Just teaching you to cover all your exits." Briar grinned, making it as friendly as possible. She couldn't give herself away now. She had to get back out to Wick. Had to formulate a plan.

Marigold laughed again, wiping her skirts. She was covered in crumbs from the bread she had been handling, a carrot peel stuck to her wrist from the vegetables she had been cutting when Briar went out to the waterfall.

"I guess you didn't stay long," Marigold said, nodding at Briar's wet feet and damp pants. "Did your Skullstalker—?"

Briar cut her off. "What did we agree you'd call the apothecary? Back when we were kids."

Marigold paused, her hands tightening in her crumb-dusted skirts. Then they forcibly loosened.

Need to keep an eye on body language, Briar thought. *I told you that, Marigold. You brushed me off.*

"The Cottage Away from Home," Marigold said, her smile genuinely soft. "You would get a friends and family discount for any potion you needed."

"And sleep in the spare room anytime," Briar

finished. She tucked the hairpin into her pocket and strolled up, careful to keep her posture loose and easy as she walked. "Because I always have a home at the cottage."

Marigold nodded. Her smile stiffened, her gaze dropping as Briar got closer.

"So," Marigold said. "Where did your Skullstalker go?"

"He's still washing. Getting that mountain smell off him; he's a little strange about it." Briar leaned on the doorway, making Marigold step out of the way. "I'm really happy for you, Marigold. You're finally getting your dream. You just need to finish this one last job."

"Right." Marigold didn't look at her. Her smile was wobbling, like she was waiting for Briar to ask exactly what that job was. She'd never gotten specific about it when Briar asked before.

But Briar said nothing. She just pulled Marigold into a hug, ignoring when Marigold stiffened.

"That friends and family discount better be huge," she said into Marigold's shoulder.

Marigold laughed nervously. "Of course! Of course. Anything for you."

Briar inhaled deeply. There, underneath the smell of bread and vegetables, was the barely-there scent of lipseed, lingering on Marigold's puffy hair.

Betrayal curled through Briar, as sharp as a stab wound.

"Oh," Marigold said, leaning back. "I almost forgot. I

just put the flower in to marinate. We should be able to remove your curses tomorrow! Isn't that wonderful?"

"Yes," Briar said, her smile aching. "I can't wait."

Wick met her as soon as she stepped out of the front door. His loincloth was damp with river water, knotted messily, as if in a hurry.

"I am sorry," he said.

He had been listening in. Or maybe he could just tell from her expression. Or he could *fucking* smell it on her, the keen-nose bastard. He'd known her for a few weeks and saw past her better than any man ever could, and it infuriated her.

"We can leave," Wick offered. "If she is not truly planning to un-curse us, we can find somewhere else. We still have your amulet, maybe some other witch—"

Briar grabbed his horns and dragged him into a kiss. She had to jump a little to do it, but Wick bent down easily, grunting into her mouth.

It was not an entirely pleasurable grunt. Briar drew back, annoyed.

"Shit," she said. "Am I hurting you?"

Wick shook his head.

"Good." Briar hauled herself up with his horns, wrapping her legs around his loincloth-clad waist. "Fuck me as hard as you can manage."

Wick's fiery eyes swelled. He had been insisting that he had healed enough to take her "properly," but for now, Briar stayed on top. Even when the blood frenzy had started to take over, it never lasted long enough for him to turn her over and rut her like an animal. The amulet was cracked and flickering, but it still worked.

For now.

Wick carried her to a shady spot near the waterfall and set her down in the grass.

Briar didn't check if Marigold would be able to see them. There were several windows on this side of the cottage, so she would probably be able to see them. But Briar couldn't bring herself to care. If Marigold was handing her into some bounty hunter's jaws, she could see Wick's entire dick for all Briar cared.

Not that she particularly wanted that. She had been surprised that she was oddly possessive of Wick when he disrobed at the altar in Yedzeva. She had the brief urge to tug her fur coat over them both and keep Wick to herself. But the villagers had wanted a show, and she had given it to them.

There was no one to put on a show for here. Just Wick and his fiery gaze fixed so strongly on her that she forgot to perform at all—a rarity she was still getting used to.

"There is a spell," Wick grunted as he thrust into her, all the way to the third ridge. "That can make you take me. Your body will rearrange itself but leave you unaltered, after."

Briar panted, open-mouthed, against the grass. She was facedown with Wick crouched over her, his arm bracing against her chest. She was obviously rubbing against his healing burns, but he showed no signs of stopping or pushing her away. Like crushing her close was worth the pain it caused him.

"How—" Briar cut off with a gasp, the ridges of his cock lighting sparks under her skin. "How m-many spells are you going to cast on me, big boy?"

"As many as it takes," Wick growled. "I want you. All of you, always."

Briar curled her hands in the grass, her clit throbbing as she imagined it: Wick getting some warlock to cast spells on his little human so she could stay at his side, taking him inhumanly deep whenever he wanted.

Wick reached down and rubbed her clit. His giant finger was so gentle, as always. Briar yelled and came, clutching the arm he had clamped around her middle. He fucked her through it, his hips stuttering as she squeezed around him.

Briar could feel herself drooling as the orgasm faded. If she walked away from this, she would spend the rest of her life chasing the high that Wick had given her. No man could compare once she had a Skullstalker.

Wick grunted, his hot breath clouding over her hair. He thrust twice more and came, pulsing inside her.

Briar petted his arm, waiting for him to pull out. But Wick only nuzzled her hair, keeping his shaking arm braced against the ground so he didn't fall and crush her.

"I am almost glad for my injuries," he confessed.

It took Briar a moment to acknowledge this. She was too distracted by the Skullstalker cock stretching her, even while soft, and his heavy weight over her. Wick had a way of blocking out the world in the sweetest way she'd ever experienced.

"You were burned to a crisp," she slurred. "How are you glad?"

"I am not a *crisp*." Wick pulled out of her with a reluctant noise and then rolled onto his back, gathering her in his arms. "It meant we had more days on this journey."

Briar said nothing and watched the sky. Wick's chin was resting against her head, his grip firm as he held her against him.

I want all of you, he had said. *Always.*

Briar had heard similar things when she was in a man's bed. But Wick did not make promises he never intended to keep.

She groaned softly. "You really mean it, huh? You want me to stay with you."

"I do," Wick said instantly, like it was easy. "Nobody has mattered to me like you. Nobody has protected me like you, nor taken care of me. No one has trusted me as you have."

Briar's eyes burned with tears. She twisted in his arms and braced herself above him.

He was watching her, careful and earnest as ever.

Briar sorely wanted to laugh at him. To tell him that wasn't how the world worked. To insist he was naive, that everyone left in the end, that she would be doing him a favor by leaving him high and dry after they found some way to undo their curses if Marigold fell through like they suspected.

But there was another part of her, slowly growing larger throughout their journey, that wanted to give him all the kindness he'd given her and more.

Maybe she had protected him like no one else. Trusted him, taken care of him, and everything else he had said.

But he'd done the same for her, too.

Briar had guarded her heart so completely, and he had broken down all her walls like they were nothing. Then he had cupped her heart so softly she almost forgot he had claws.

She opened her mouth, unsure what she would say.

Then something cracked, the noise loud enough to make them both jump.

They both looked down. The amulet hung between them, flickering with spasmodic white light. It was even joltier than before, barely lasting a blink before it faded.

"Shit." Briar clutched it desperately, holding it so they could both look at it.

The crack along the amulet was growing. Soon, it would reach the other side and shatter into two.

Another flicker of white flashed and then died. It was different from past flashes; those were bright and clear. This looked... strange. Patchy. Almost like there were flickers of snow inside.

A window opened on the other side of the cottage. Briar recognized its specific creak: it was the kitchen. Another room she had snuck through, that time when

Marigold had locked the door and Briar was drunk and too tired to keep knocking.

"Um," Marigold called into the forest. "If you're finished, dinner is almost ready!"

The window closed.

Briar sighed, slumping against Wick's chest.

"She says she'll undo our curses tomorrow," she announced.

Wick stroked her back. "Do you think she will?"

Briar considered. She didn't *have* to say it would happen tomorrow. That meant that either Marigold was making good on her promise, or something very different was going to happen.

"I think we need a plan," Briar said.

Twenty

Marigold started the counter-curse as the dawn bled over the mountains.

"Perfect time to undo a curse," Marigold said as they set everything up. She spun her staff so rapidly that both Wick and Briar had to step out of the way multiple times, and she stunk so strongly of fear-sweat that Wick thought even Briar could smell it.

Marigold jumped from foot to foot, still spinning her staff. "Briar! Would you step into the circle?"

Briar looked up from the circle Marigold had made her carve into the grass. She looked over at Wick and then slotted her knife back into its holster and stepped into the circle.

"In the circle," Briar reported. "What next, magic lady?"

"One second." Marigold twirled her staff thoughtfully, examining the circle. "What am I missing.... Oh!"

She bent down to the golden bowl sitting at the top

of the circle and conjured a spark to drop into the bowl. The bowl burst into flame, glowing in the dawn light.

Wick watched the bowl of flames warily. Briar caught him looking and frowned.

"You won't get burned this time," she assured him.

Wick appreciated it. Even though he had not been worried about being burned, only what Marigold had been planning to do to Briar. It was her ritual, after all. They still did not know whether this was a ruse or not. The moment Briar seemed like she was in pain, Wick would leap into action.

But nothing seemed amiss. Marigold seemed genuinely like she was setting up a spell to remove her friend's curse. Despite her nervous sweating and constant staff-spinning.

"What is that fire, anyhow?" Briar asked. "It looks... different."

"It's purified for the ritual," said Marigold distractedly. "It will burn through anything. Do *not* touch it."

"Wasn't planning to," Briar said with another glance toward Wick.

"Okay," Marigold said to herself. She held the staff in front of her and closed her eyes. "Okay, okay, okay. We can do this. Briar, stay still."

Wick met Briar's eyes questioningly and took a small step toward the circle.

Briar hesitated. Then she shook her head.

Wick stood back.

Marigold took a long, deep breath and opened her eyes.

Wick held back a gasp. Her eyes were icy white, snow swirling inside them. He had seen that before. He had seen that last night, in the cracked amulet around Briar's neck.

Briar's eyebrows raised. But before either of them could say anything, Marigold spoke.

"*Utîngu mî utîtwefach wim mî pe*," she whispered, her voice like a faraway mountain breeze.

The fire swelled inside the bowl. A white light bloomed from it, curling around Briar's arms and legs and twisting around her body.

Briar gave Wick a panicked look. But when Wick stepped forward, she shook her head again.

Wick stilled reluctantly. He watched the white light pulse as it crept toward her chest, climbing inexorably toward her heart.

"*Vyâng fto fwâng mîk,*" Marigold cried. "*Mîk, mîk, mîk!*"

The flames climbed so high they almost touched the branches hanging overhead. The light hit Briar's heart and exploded, showering the circle in a sea of white sparks.

Wick stumbled forward. But when the light faded, the fire was settling, and Briar was standing in the circle, unharmed. Her hands were clasped over her chest, her eyes tracking.

"Briar," Wick said urgently.

Briar met his eyes with a disbelieving smile. "I-I can't feel the heat anymore. I think—"

"It worked," Marigold yelled. She clapped joyously,

twirling her staff. Then she sagged to the side, looking like she was about to pass out on the grass.

Briar leapt out of the circle to steady her. "Hey, hey, hey! Don't go to sleep yet. Still one more curse to break."

"Yes," Marigold said weakly. She straightened, checking first on the bowl of fire, which was burning merrily beside her.

It took her a moment to spin to Wick. "And now you."

Wick's relief turned once more into suspicion. She stank of fear, but it was not all toward him.

Marigold wiped her sweaty hands on her skirt and then swore. "Damn, I forgot the chains!"

"Chains," Briar repeated. She was still rubbing her chest through her shirt. "Why do you need chains?"

Marigold waved her hand dismissively, not looking at her. "Oh, you know! Just in case the counter-curse doesn't work, and he goes feral."

She turned toward the cottage.

Briar stepped in front of her, blocking her way. "Is that an option?"

Marigold paused for a moment too long before laughing. "Hopefully not!"

She stepped around Briar, her smile rigid and desperate. But before she could take another step toward the cottage, she made a mistake:

She glanced up at the trees.

Wick tilted his head up and gave an imperceptible sniff. A breeze blew in his direction, bringing the unmistakable scent of lipseed in the air.

Wick surged forward and grabbed Marigold's wrist.

Marigold spluttered. She tugged at Wick's grip, staring at Briar in panic.

"What is he *doing*?" she hissed.

Briar said nothing. She did not even look at Wick as she strolled up to Marigold, her gait deceivingly casual despite the hard edge in her eyes.

"Briar!" Marigold whimpered. She drew her staff back like she was going to hit him with it. "Tell him I'm only trying to help!"

"You're not *helping* him," Briar said flatly. "You're restraining him so you can *sell* me, you backstabbing, lying, void-rotted little shit."

"That's— That's not—" Marigold stared at Briar with a terrified smile, stiff with shock. Then her head snapped up toward the trees. "RENAULT! NOW!"

A familiar voice swore from the treetops. Renault launched himself from the branches, coming to a rolling stop on the ground. He was battered and bandaged, but otherwise whole.

Marigold whirled on Wick, her staff raised. Not to strike him, Wick realized all too late, but to cast a spell on him.

"*Nyaankhī*," she cried.

Ice burst from the ground and surrounded him, digging into his skin. Wick released Marigold, attempting to claw the ice off, but it climbed thick over his arms and up his chest until he was frozen in place.

"Wick!" Briar yelled.

Wick grunted. The ice was sharp and painfully cold,

pressing into his chin. But no further. Marigold strained beside him, her staff still outstretched.

Behind her stood Renault the bounty hunter, a crossbow raised at Briar's heart.

"Briar," Wick warned.

Briar gritted her teeth. Even through the overwhelming stench of ice and Marigold's nervous sweat, he could smell Briar's fury—hot and blazing, so overpowering it almost masked her devastating worry.

Briar unsheathed her knife and turned reluctantly to face Renault. "All alone, huh? Looks like someone killed your team."

Renault scowled. His hair looked limper than usual. There was a bandage showing above his collar, and his pale skin was covered in a fine sheen of sweat. Briar's knife must have gotten him deep.

"If you don't mind," Renault said thinly. "I'm a little tired of our usual back-and-forth. Marigold, your coin as promised."

Crossbow still aloft, he pulled a cloth bag from his belt. It was bulging, and it took Wick a painful moment to realize where he knew it from: this was the bag of gold he had stolen from the ritual.

Briar pointed her blade at it. "That's mine."

"Finders fucking keepers," Renault spat.

He dropped the bag. Both women's eyes fell with it, their eyes alight with want.

Renault pulled the trigger. Wick roared, ice cracking around him as he fought against the witch's hold.

Briar leapt out of the way. The arrow ripped her

shirt, leaving a line of blood on her waist before tunneling into a tree behind them.

Marigold grunted. Her hands flexed around her staff, ice thickening to cover the cracks Wick had placed in it.

Wick glared at her. He could get out if given enough time. But they needed to break her concentration long enough for him to do so.

"Shit," Renault hissed. He reloaded the crossbow, but it was too late. Briar was already running at him, her knife poised to strike.

Wick watched helplessly as they clashed, Renault using the crossbow as a blunt weapon as he attempted to load it. Briar dodged him yet again and drove the knife toward his throat, only to be shoved away by a sharp elbow.

Wick had never seen humans fight with such grace. All his fighting had been savage, half-remembered, and brief. Watching them almost looked like a dance. A horrible, deadly dance he could not tear his eyes away from as Briar grunted and ducked, trying desperately to sink her blade into Renault's sweaty skin.

Wick attempted to move his arms. The ice strained and cracked around his bulging muscles, only to be replaced by another layer as Marigold braced herself against her staff.

"Help me," Renault barked as he shoved away yet another of Briar's knife attacks. "Damn it, witch! Help me or lose your coin!"

Marigold gasped, shaking with effort. "I-I have to hold the spell! Or he'll get free!"

"He's covered in ice, what will he do? If you don't start helping me right *now*—" Renault stopped, bellowing in pain. Briar had finally landed a blow, her knife striking him across the cheek.

Renault stumbled back, wiping his bleeding face.

"Void take you, you rancid whore!" He kicked Briar in the chest, sending her sprawling backward. Then he lurched sideways to grab the bag of gold and threw it mightily, sending it sailing toward the burning bowl from Briar's ritual, its flames glowing unnaturally.

Marigold screamed. "NO!"

The bag struck the bowl and burst, showering gold into the fire. It immediately began to melt, liquid gold filling the bowl as the flames burned.

Marigold whirled, heaving her staff away from Wick and redirecting her ice efforts toward the bowl. She even staggered toward it, wobbling with exertion.

Wick called on all his strength. He flexed, and the ice cracked around his right arm, then his left. But it still wasn't enough. Marigold was grabbing the few coins that had fallen out of the bowl, but Renault was growing steadier on his feet.

"Alright," he panted at Briar. "Now— Hey!"

Briar ran at Wick and slammed the hilt of her knife into the center of his ice-clad chest.

A loud *crack* rang through the trees. The ice shattered, falling off of Wick in huge, freezing chunks.

"That's more like it," Briar said breathlessly. She slotted her knife back into its holster and asked, "You with me, big boy?"

"Always," Wick replied.

He kicked the remaining ice off his feet and turned to Renault, who looked like he deeply regretted his actions.

"Now, hold on," Renault began.

Wick lunged at him. Renault cursed and raised his crossbow, shooting wildly.

The arrow whizzed uselessly over Wick's head. He knocked the crossbow out of Renault's hands and pinned him to the ground by his chest. He made sure to press hard on the stab wound Briar had given him in Yedzeva, digging his claws into the surrounding flesh.

Renault cried out in pain. "Wait! Don't kill me! I can tell them you're dead, that we can't recover the body! They trust me, they'll believe whatever I say!"

Wick looked over at Briar, who hummed consideringly. Her chest was heaving from the fight, but she did not smell wounded. That was good. If she were, Wick would have killed him without waiting for Briar's permission.

"Or," Briar said, swiping her sweaty hair out of her face. "We send a letter from your last surviving team member saying you confirmed my death and want the reward, with a strip of my hair as proof—"

"What?" Renault said weakly.

"But, oh no, you died tragically in an animal attack before you could come to claim it," Briar continued. "Wick?"

Wick lunged and dug his fangs into Renault's throat.

Renault screamed. It quickly turned into wet gurgles as Wick pulled back, stringy flesh connecting his mouthful to the shredded remains of Renault's neck.

Blood gushed onto the grass. Wick swallowed his lump of meat and ignored the blood frenzy burning at the edges of his mind, slowly heating him up.

Renault let out a final gasp and went still. Briar pressed her boot into his cheek, testing for a reaction. He did not move as she kicked his limp hair over his forehead.

"That's him dealt with," she said. She gripped the cracked amulet and turned to Wick. "How are you feeling?"

Wick licked his bloody mouth. The burning was growing hotter inside his skull.

"I am myself," he said. "For now."

Briar gave him a short nod and turned to the bowl of fire behind them.

Marigold was crouched next to it. At first, Wick thought she was groping for the scant few coins that had fallen into the grass. Then he realized she was attempting to push herself up and failing, her arms shaking from all her magic.

"Wait," she croaked. "Briar, you don't understand!"

"I don't? Because it looks like you screwed me over so you could get your fucking apothecary," Briar snarled. She gestured at Wick to step forward.

Wick did. Then he hesitated. Briar still stank of fury, but there was so much sorrow underneath it now that she was looking at her old friend.

"You remember how we grew up," Marigold blurted.

"You remember how many nights we went hungry, all those things we had to do to survive!"

"Yes, and then you went to your cozy magic palace while I starved on the streets," Briar said coolly. "Is this meant to make me pity you? Because it isn't working."

Marigold shook her head, eyes gleaming with tears. "Things have been *hard* out here! I just want to feel safe. You understand, you *must* understand. That's all you want, isn't it? To finally have enough money to feel *safe.*"

Briar's mouth twitched bitterly.

"I don't know what you mean," she said, and Wick knew it was a lie. "I want so many riches, I choke on them. Speaking of choking..."

She nodded at Wick. Wick looked back at her beseechingly. The blood frenzy was building, and it wanted nothing more than for him to give himself over to the violence Briar was offering. But he could sense her hesitance even if he couldn't smell the sadness wafting off of her in waves.

"Wait," Marigold cried. She shuffled back, her fists full of coins she had managed to salvage from the grass. "Wait, don't! Help me!"

She tipped her head up to the sky. The temperature dropped so suddenly that even Wick noticed it, and Briar shivered.

"My lord Titan," Marigold screamed. "Save me!"

At first, Wick thought the sensation running through him was shock. Then Briar shuddered, and he realized it was a tide running through the forest, rushing into Marigold with such force her head snapped back with it.

Marigold's mouth dropped open. A white light glowed within it, filling her eyes and lifting her from the ground. Wind ran through the trees, cold and biting, so forceful it made Briar stumble into him.

"What's happening?" Briar demanded.

Wick steadied her and shook his head. The burn in his skull was flaring hotter than ever, and yet the cold felt so familiar.

"I guess she really is a warlock," Briar yelled over the howling wind. She looked up at him, shielding her eyes. "Titan! Isn't that—?"

The wind died down so suddenly that Briar fell silent in the middle of her sentence.

Marigold hovered above them, her limbs dangling uselessly at her sides. Her glowing face was tipped up to the sky. No, not the sky, Wick realized, but to the mountains.

Marigold's mouth did not move. But the voice that echoed around the trees could come from nothing else.

"*Hello, child,*" said the voice that had been whispering in Wick's mind since before he could remember.

Wick stepped in front of Briar protectively, curling his remaining wing around her. "Titan. You speak to me, to many of us. Why?"

The voice hummed. "*We are the old instincts. There is not much left of us. Only corpse bones sticking up from the ground, only whispers in your head. You have made us louder. We thank you.*"

Briar nudged him from where she was peeking out from behind him. "*Corpse bones*? Are you saying they're the *mountains*—wait, not important. Wick, ask if they can fix you!"

The voice made a noise like rocks cracking.

"*Fix*," it repeated curiously.

Wick's skin crawled. He held Briar tighter to him and said, "I am plagued by a blood frenzy which makes me kill all I see. This amulet, the witch infused it with you. It is the only thing that calms the frenzy."

The thing that was once Marigold's head lolled. It was many moments before it spoke.

"*No*," it said simply.

"No," Wick repeated. "No, it is not you?"

"*It is us*," it rasped. "*But we will not rid you of your primal instincts. You are the purest Skullstalker still living.*"

"Pure?" Wick demanded. "I am *cursed*! Even now, it invades my head. I can feel it burning inside me. I don't want—"

He looked down at Briar, the words sticking in his throat as she looked back at him with those big, bright eyes. He had said the words so many times, but never more than right now.

"I do not wish to hurt anyone," he whispered.

He touched the amulet hanging over her shirt. Briar covered his hand, squeezing gently.

The voice boomed through the trees. "*There is nothing wrong with you, child. In fact, there is something very right inside you. Many eons ago, all Skullstalkers were like you. Born to wage our wars. Then, at the end, the defects began. All of your Skullstalkers are wrong... except for you. Your 'blood frenzy,' as you call it, is your species in its purest form."*

Wick reeled. He had lived his whole life knowing only the scant history his brothers told him, a history even their eldest were unsure of. But none of them had ever suggested this.

"Wick?" Briar asked uncertainly. Her hand was so warm over his, rubbing comfortingly.

"No," Wick said. "That is not true. I would— We would know."

"You were created to destroy," the voice continued. *"This is what you were meant to be. Beautiful destruction."*

"But the amulet," Wick tried. He opened his hand, revealing its dull glory. It had cracked even further since last night. His only hope—and it was breaking.

"A mortal mistake," the voice said. *"Nothing more. Goodbye, child."*

"Shit," Briar whispered. "Hey, wait! You can't leave like this!"

She took a step toward the floating Marigold. But Wick was faster, bounding up and seizing her, dragging her down to look her in her glowing face.

"If this is the nature you placed in me," he hissed, his voice distorting with the blood fury welling inside him, "then I refuse my nature! I am not what you made me!"

"We can sense it," the voice told him, maddeningly calm. *"We feel it burn. The fire swells."*

"And it is not *me*," Wick roared. "I am not this

relentless, savage thing unless I will it! I am choice! I am
—I—"

He stuttered to a stop. His head throbbed with heat,
the blood frenzy threatening to take over.

Briar rushed to his side. He tried to hold her back,
but she ducked under his wing and grabbed his chin.

"Look at me," she said, trying to force him to look
down. "Hey! Wick! Eyes on me, big boy. Don't give in."

"Run," Wick managed. "Hurt me. Do whatever you
must."

"I'm not leaving you," Briar insisted.

Wick tried to tell her again to run. But the only thing
that came from his throat was a roar, rough and hungry.
His claws burst from his fingers, digging into the Titan's
arms. A red tinge enveloped the world. He could only
hope that he devoured Marigold's body first, giving Briar
enough time to flee.

The being that was once Marigold glowed brighter,
the white light bleeding red.

"You are ours," the voice said.

Wick squeezed his eyes shut. The world disappeared,
leaving only a wild pounding of his own blood through
his veins, telling him to strike, to hurt, to *kill*.

But there was something underneath it. Something
small and stubborn and beautiful, even when she was
tired or pained or sleeping.

She did not run. She had stayed with him, her voice
cutting through his frenzy. She was saying many things,
but only one word made it through:

"Wick."

Wick growled, prying his eyes open to meet those of the glowing Titan's.

"I am not yours," he managed, the word thick and thorny. "I am HERS!"

His grip tightened. The Titan's arms broke underneath his hands, its flimsy mortal bones splintering.

"*Good*," the Titan said. *"Let it consume you. Become what you were always meant to be."*

"Let me show you," Wick demanded. "Let me show you what I am, what I truly am. You will see."

With every piece of will he had left, he pressed his forehead to the Titan's.

The Titan paused. *"Very well."*

Its glow was so bright it made his eyes water, even when he closed them. Still, he stayed, Briar's voice finally fading as the Titan did as he asked.

The world fell away. He could feel the Titan groping through his head, watching his memories with detached curiosity:

The first time he attempted to make a friend, a frog he dubbed Froggy, who met an untimely end on Wick's claws. The first time that he was chased out of a village. His first nest, covered in as much softness as he could find. Waking up time after time from a blood frenzy, the anguish fading to quiet disappointment after so many centuries.

Then, finally: Briar. The shock in her gorgeous eyes as he instructed her to hurt him. The delicious stretch of her hole, the contentment of curling up around her in sleep. Her wary gaze, filled with disbelief and lust and finally trust. The bliss of tasting her, of feeling her tighten around him. Her tearful eyes as he told her to hurt him once again in the ravine. Her careful hands rubbing cream into his burns, feeding him rabbit, and tending to him with a care no one had ever shown him.

He wanted to keep her safe. But mostly, he wanted to keep her. And the Titan saw all of it, every small second.

At the end of his memories, the Titan sighed in disappointment.

You really should have eaten her, it said inside his head.

Then it withdrew. Wick stumbled, the forest flooding back into place around him as he righted himself.

Briar grabbed his side, as if her small stature could help. "Wick! Are you alright? What happened? Your eyes were glowing!"

"I am fine," he assured her.

He blinked hard. The red haze was dimming, but the frenzy was still there. He could feel it at the edges of his mind, waiting.

"Please," Wick rasped. "You can do it. I know you can."

The Titan drifted from his grasp. Its skin was broken, light showing between the gaps. It looked down at him, its glowing eyes fixed on its creation.

At first, Wick thought it would forsake him. He could feel its contempt, in the end. But its next words were not a condemnation; it was a command.

"Break the amulet," it said.

Wick looked down at Briar, who clutched the amulet protectively.

"You are not worthy to be one of my children," the Titan continued. *"None of you are. You will not hear from me again."*

The light bled from its eyes and mouth and into its skin. It pulsed, light cracking through its skin until the being that was once Marigold dissolved into a flurry of light.

Wick covered his and Briar's eyes with his wing. By the time the light faded, Marigold was nothing but motes of light fading into the trees.

Briar reached up to touch a dying speck of light. As soon as it touched her finger, it vanished.

Briar rubbed her fingers together. The scent of grief clung to her, thick and heady.

"Briar," Wick tried. He placed a hand on her shoulder. "I am sorry."

Briar moved like she was going to shrug him off. Instead, she reached up and snapped the amulet off its chain.

"Do we trust it?" she asked. "The Titan?"

"I do not think we have a choice," Wick admitted.

They stared at the amulet sitting in Briar's hand. It was so close to splitting in two. The barest hint of pressure would do it.

"Well," Briar said. "Here goes nothing."

Wick held out his hand. Briar placed her hand inside his. They closed their fingers, Wick's pressing against Briar's until he felt the amulet split in two.

Light burst out of the shattered amulet, flooding straight into Wick.

Wick gasped, the breath punched out of him. He fell to his knees as it rolled through him, cold and cleansing. Ice flooded through his skull, all the way to the ends of his claw tips and back to circle his heart.

Then it *clenched*.

When Wick came to, he was lying on his back in the grass. Briar was kneeling over him, stroking his face.

"Hi," she croaked, her eyes wet. "How are we feeling? Still wanting to rip the flesh from my bones?"

Wick shook his head. He felt... clear. There were no embers left in him. The ice had frozen the burning frenzy out of him for good.

"It is gone," he said, hardly daring to believe it.

Briar broke into a grin. She was half-crying, haloed by morning light, and the most beautiful thing Wick had ever seen.

He touched her cheek. "You gave up your coin."

Briar frowned, like she did not know what he meant. Then her expression cleared. She laughed, disbelievingly, and dropped her forehead against his.

"You broke your nature for me," she said. "It was the least I could do for my gentleman monster."

With that, she wiped the blood away from his mouth and kissed him. She tasted like every morning for the rest of Wick's long life.

Eighty-Seven Years Later

Briar spent the afternoon doing her favorite post-lunch activity:

Taking all four ridges of her Skullstalker husband's cock.

Briar twisted to wink at him, her cheek pressing into the deer fur that lined their nest. "Is that all you've got, big boy?"

Wick growled a laugh, his hips working hard. He looked beautiful like this, framed in the afternoon light streaming through the cottage window. Briar let herself look for a moment longer before a particularly deep thrust made her eyes flutter shut.

He was curled over her, pressing her face into the furs while he fucked her from behind. It was where they often ended up. Briar would begin by riding him, then tease him until he couldn't take it anymore. Then he would take charge, folding her into whatever position he wished and pounding her until he came.

It hadn't taken long after they uncursed themselves for them to find their way to a spell that would let Briar take all of him. And increase her lifespan, of course. Briar was the proud owner of a lifespan spanning several millennia, and a body that could take every gorgeous inch of Wick's cock.

Wick's tail curled around her waist, holding her in place as he thrust harder. "Tell me how it feels."

"It feels—" Briar panted into the fur, her eyelids fluttering. Every thrust made her light up inside, her body stretching impossibly to fill him. The first time he finally fit that fourth ridge inside her, she had actually cried with relief. Sometimes she still felt like that, all the relief and triumph and *love* overflowing until he wiped it away with a gentle claw.

"Feels like I'm going to die if you don't come in me," she managed. "Feels like it all the time, every gods-damned day. I *need* it."

"I know," Wick soothed. "I will give it to you, my lovely thief."

It took barely two passes of his huge finger over her clit before Briar was coming, crying out against the furs as she spasmed around him. He fucked her through it, turning each wave of bliss so overwhelming that Briar was hardly aware of what she was saying. But it must have been sappy, because when she pried her eyes open again, his big, black, fiery eyes were softer than ever.

"So tight," he panted. "So perfect. Made for me."

"All for you," Briar slurred. She pulled his finger up and sucked it into her mouth, feeling his hips stutter against her. She closed her eyes, letting herself enjoy those ridges slamming into her oversensitive hole, then pulled his finger out of her mouth.

"Come on, big boy," she said. "Mate me."

Wick shuddered and came, his remaining wing flaring out with such majesty it took Briar's breath away. He pulsed inside her, his tail tightening around her waist so tightly that Briar knew it would cause marks.

Then he went boneless, slumping next to her in the nest. He reached out blindly, and Briar let herself get tucked into his side.

For a time, they just lay there, the afternoon light coating their naked bodies. But after a while, Briar yawned.

"The Emmett brothers are coming around soon," she announced. "I think I should put on some clothes."

Wick rumbled a disagreement against her ribs. But he made no move to stop her as she sat up, stretching.

"We turned down their last two contracts," he pointed out.

"So? Maybe this time they'll have something exciting." Briar flashed him a smile and stroked his wing stub, which stretched fondly toward her. It had taken her many years to be able to touch it without guilt, but she had gotten there eventually. With a lot of assurance from Wick, who always insisted that she could cut off his remaining wing if she ever needed to.

"Never know what the day will hold," Briar told him, getting up in search of clothes.

· · ·

Not long after, the two of them sat on the porch they had built and looked at the waterfall.

They had taken over Marigold's cottage after they removed their curses. They had trashed most of the clutter and rebuilt several walls until the cottage could fit Wick comfortably, then settled in for some well-earned peace and quiet.

But the quiet life, it turned out, was only fun for so long. While Briar did love her peace, she did need the occasional adventure every once in a while. And Wick was more than happy to indulge her.

He raised his head, sniffing the forest air.

"The Emmett brothers are close," he announced.

Briar hummed. She held out a bottle of elderberry cider, and Wick popped it open with one easy claw.

"Speaking of brothers," Briar said once she had taken a sip of the cool, clear cider. "Let's go see your brother Slate soon."

Wick huffed a laugh. "You are only asking because you want to do that job in the Crystal Wastes with Ruby."

"I can't help it if your brother's wife is fun," Briar argued joyously. "And you have to admit, having a half-god along on the job *does* make it easier."

Wick snorted. Then he sat up, his fiery eyes fixed on the trees.

Briar waited. Sure enough, the Emmett brothers emerged. The oldest one, William, waved. The younger one, Emery, slunk behind him with a bag over his shoulder, as cautious as ever. Emery was young, perhaps five and twenty, and still hadn't completely shaken off his fear of the ageless, monstrous couple who lived at the edge of the forest.

But at least he hadn't come with torches and pitch-forks. Those bloodthirsty groups had been popular for a year or two, and Briar didn't like it. Wick was always so sad while she washed their blood off of him.

"Lady Thief," William called. "You look well."

Briar waved back at them. "Will! Good to see the baby's finally being brought into the fold. About time he sharpened his teeth."

"He's getting the hang of it," William replied. He tilted his hat at Wick. "Mister Skullstalker! Always a pleasure."

"And to you," Wick replied, amused. William was the latest in a surprisingly strong line of mortals who called Wick their friend, a fact that Wick was still getting used to.

The younger brother, Emery, cleared his throat.

"We come with offerings," called Emery timidly.

William rolled his eyes. "You don't have to announce it, you dolt. They can see the bag."

He whacked the aforementioned bag hanging over Emery's shoulder. Emery heaved it to the ground, revealing gold coins, woven blankets, and a fish paste that Wick enjoyed.

Briar looked at Wick. He inhaled deeply and nodded.

"Good lads," Briar called. "I do love it when you stop in Hasterville; Wick can't get enough of that fish stuff. What job do you have for us?"

"There is a town up north that requests help," William declared. "They are beset upon by pixies. They said you helped them before?"

Briar groaned, stirring her cider with a long spoon. "We told them to keep the wards up. Wick, didn't we tell them?"

"We told them," Wick said. "But it has been a mortal generation. They will have forgotten."

"Damn mortals and their damn lifespans," Briar muttered. She straightened in her chair and considered. It was a *long* trek. They had just finished planting the tomatoes in the vegetable garden. And Briar didn't particularly want to sleep rough for so long.

She turned to Wick and found him watching her intently. Anything she said, he would do.

Briar gave him a fond smile and turned back to the Emmett brothers.

"You two can take care of it," she said.

William's brows rose. "You have been turning down many of our quests lately. Is the Lady Thief getting a bit long in the tooth?"

Briar laughed, enjoying how panicked it made Emery look. "Excuse me for thinking you two can handle a simple pixie job on your own!"

"You have our trust," Wick said. "Tell them we sent you. They will reward you richly."

William hesitated. He seemed on the verge of a question. Then he bowed, barely an inclination of his head compared to the low bow his little brother sank into.

"That means a lot," he said, and Briar could hear the

sincerity despite his cocky smirk. "We will report back when the matter is solved."

"Stay safe," Wick said.

"And you." William gave them another brisk nod, his eyes full of questions that Briar still denied him after all their years of working together. Then he strode back through the trees, his brother on his tail.

Briar went back to stirring her cider. It was homemade, yet another hobby Wick had picked up since settling down. Cider-making and making ornaments out of animal skulls: two of his favorite pastimes in the last decades.

"That makes three jobs you have turned down," Wick told her.

Briar sipped her cider and shrugged. "Who can be bothered traveling all that way? Besides, I'd miss home."

She could feel his eyes on her. But she still waited until he leaned over to her chair and picked her up, depositing her in his lap.

"Oh?" he said warmly.

Briar lifted her glass. "You made me spill my cider."

He stuck his long tongue out and ran the tip along the glass, cleaning up the drop that had rolled down the surface.

"Am I forgiven?" he asked coyly.

Briar held back a smile. She leaned her head against his shoulder, gazing up at him as the waterfall bubbled in the background.

"Next time, we will go with them," she said. "Right

now... I just want some comfort. Can you give that to me?"

Wick growled, low and satisfied, and lowered his forehead to hers. The cool, scarred bone felt like walking through the cottage door after a long job and taking off her shoes, finally ready to relax.

"I will do my best," Wick purred and winked.

Briar grinned. There had been no whispers from the mountains in all their years together. No blood frenzy beating at the edges of his skull. Just peace, plain and simple. Even on the most dangerous jobs, they could still find their peace together.

Wick wrapped her up in his arms.

Briar closed her eyes and let their hard-won peace wash over her.

Epilogue

This bonus epilogue for HELD is a stretch goal unlocked by the lovely backers of the BOUND Kickstarter campaign!

Wick had never been blindfolded before.

"It's going to be great," Briar called as he stumbled blindly through the fields. "Nearly there.... Almost... Okay, take it off!"

Wick pulled the blindfold away, relieved to see it was only lightly singed from his repeated attempts to open his fiery eyes. Then he blinked, shocked at the sight awaiting him: a giant woven basket attached to an even bigger balloon, with a flame flickering at the open base.

Briar beamed, throwing out her arms.

"Happy anniversary," she yelled.

"It is…" Wick trailed off, cocking his head. "What *is* it?"

"It's a hot air balloon!" Briar bound up to him and reached up in a clear sign that she wanted to be carried. He scooped her up obediently, and she slung her arms around his neck.

"I showed you a sketch in that book a few years ago," Briar said. "Remember? On the Hachetfield job. Before we set off the basilisk trap."

"Ah," Wick said. "The inventor's sketchbook. I do remember."

Briar's smile turned shy. "I had it custom-made. Extra big so we can go for a fly together."

Wick stared down at her, touched. He hadn't remembered *that* from the inventor's sketchbook. He supposed he had been distracted by the arrival of the basilisks, which had taken a chunk out of his leg before he and Briar killed them all.

He looked at the hot air balloon again. It was trying to fly, he realized. There were sandbags tied to the basket, holding it down.

Briar, apparently, took his silence as reluctance. "It's the least I could do, after all. Since I chopped off your only way to fly."

"And I am glad for it," he reminded her, curling his remaining wing around her. "I would have you cut off my other wing before I hurt you again."

Briar grinned. Even after all these centuries, her smile could still make Wick's hot heart flicker.

"Come on," Briar said, nudging her boot into his

bare belly. "Let's fly, big guy."

After climbing in and slicing the hot air balloon free of its weights, Wick took flight for the first time in three hundred years.

Slowly. Horizontally. With nothing but a basket to protect them from plummeting.

"They reinforced it for you," Briar explained as he nudged the floor of the basket with his clawed foot. "They tested it with rocks. Nobody's falling out."

Wick peered over the side. They were almost at the height of the treetops surrounding the field. If Briar fell from this height, she would be badly injured. A normal human would be dead, but Briar had not been mortal for a long time.

"How do we guide it?" Wick asked.

Briar shrugged, pulling on the rope that made the fire bigger.

"We don't," she said. "The wind does."

As if in response, the wind blew a particularly strong gust. The balloon listed sideways toward the trees.

Wick watched the ground get smaller and smaller. "How do we land?"

Briar pointed to a rope. "We release the hot air— *slowly*—and it will let us back down."

Wick rumbled, low in his throat. He was so busy looking out over the view that he didn't realize Briar was watching him until she rubbed the base of his horns.

"What do you think?" Briar asked nervously. "Pretty

good gift, right? *Way* better than the last decade. I don't know what I was thinking with that Pegasus."

"It is very nice," Wick replied. He looked around them, watching the treetops get further away. They were ascending at a surprising speed, the clouds closer than they had been in a very long time.

His wing stub throbbed. Phantom pain, as Briar called it. The injury hadn't truly ached in generations. But Wick still felt it sometimes. Especially now, when he was high in the sky and getting higher.

Briar dropped the rope and shivered, huddling against him. "Phew. Forgot how *cold* flying was."

Wick rubbed her arms, lingering on the raised bumps on her skin. She had more scars after a life with a Skull-stalker, and he loved every one of them.

Briar nuzzled her head under his chin. "Is that all you got? Warm me up *properly*, big boy."

Wick's tail flickered in surprise. He tucked a claw under her chin, tilting her head up to see her mischievous smile.

"Here?" he asked. "Truly? We are in the sky."

"I know!" Briar laughed, delighted. "We never got to sky-fuck when you had your wings. Think about it: finally, something we haven't done!"

Wick was not one to hunt out new sexual adventures, like Briar was. He was sated with what they had. But he had to admit there was a novelty to this.

He flexed his remaining wing, testing the basket's limits. "There is not much room to move. I could not take you on your knees, the way you like."

"Oh no," Briar sighed, rolling her eyes. "Guess I'll have to settle for my gentleman monster lifting me up and down on his cock."

Wick's aforementioned cock stirred under his loincloth. The material was from a previous anniversary, dark blue to offset his skin. It was silkier than anything he'd ever known before Briar, who had brought so much into his life he could never thank her enough for it. Before Briar, he lived in a cave and had no one. Now he lived in a cottage near a waterfall and had many friends, even if they had a depressing tendency to age and die too fast.

But not Briar. She would age with him, together, until he took his last breath.

Briar clung to his neck, giggling as he disrobed. She had worn a dress, a rarity for someone who preferred pants as strongly as she did. Wick should have known.

Briar reached down and took his cock, pumping it until it stood at attention. Then she spread her legs, letting him hold her by the thighs.

"Hold on," he warned her.

"I always do," Briar said breathlessly.

They both groaned as he breached her. Once upon a time, it would have taken time to open her up. He would use his tongue, then his fingers, and even then, she could only take most of his cock. But thanks to the magic his brother supplied him, Briar could take every ridge of his cock and cry out for more.

He still teased her at first. He always did. They both liked the way her mouth fell open, her eyes going hungry and pleading.

"Give me more," she said as he rocked her slowly up and down on his cockhead. "I can take it."

"Patience," he chided her. It was a game they played. He was not one to chide, but she was so pretty when she begged.

It did not take long before Briar groaned, her hips bucking, trying to take more of him.

"Come *on*," she cried. "Give it to me. Fuck me like you mean it."

Her skin was covered in goosebumps. They were climbing into the sky, and Wick barely cared. Not with his wife so tight around him, pleading for more.

He pulled her down onto his first ridge. Briar gasped, biting her lip against a grin.

"You know I can take more than that," she breathed.

He ran a claw over her thigh, pebbled with goosebumps. "You are cold."

"Then warm me up *properly*, like I *said*," she demanded.

Wick chuckled, the noise turning into a growl as he dragged her down onto the rest of his cock. All four ridges squeezed inside her, and Briar's mouth opened on a wordless cry.

Wick changed the pace, winding his arms around her to hold her still as he fucked into her.

"My beautiful wife," he growled as he pushed into her over and over. "My lovely, sweet, *generous* wife. Giving me something I thought I would never have again. How can I repay you?"

Briar laughed, the noise breaking every time he thrust inside. "Y-you know the answer to that."

Wick huffed a laugh and curled his wing around her, bringing her close enough to kiss. Then he let go of her leg, feeling her wrap it around his waist as he reached for her clit.

Briar cried out and tightened around him, her expression turning to pure bliss. There was no fear anymore; there had been no fear for centuries. Wick basked in it until his own release snuck up on him and he stilled, all four cock ridges pulsing as he emptied inside her.

For a long minute, neither of them moved. Briar hummed, rubbing her cheek against his chest. Wick stared out at the view, realizing just how far up they had gotten while they were distracted.

He could almost touch the clouds from here. It filled him with a bittersweet happiness, remembering all the times he had the same thought when he was flying.

Briar reached behind him, trailing a thoughtful hand around the long-healed wing stub she had cut through all those years ago.

"Do you miss it?" she asked.

It was not the first time she had asked. But Wick answered truthfully, as he always did.

"Sometimes," he replied. "But I love you far more than I miss it."

They said nothing for a long minute. Briar kissed his chest, then twisted to admire the view.

"Whoa," she said. "We've covered a lot of ground. I didn't realize how strong the wind was."

Wick rumbled in agreement, rubbing her back as he pulled out of her. She was no longer shivering, but that would change if they stayed up this high.

Briar climbed out of his arms and took a rope, pulling it until the balloon opened something at the top, and they started their slow descent.

Wick squinted down at the land below. They were above a forest, with no fields to be seen.

"It might take us a while to find somewhere empty enough to land," Briar admitted. "We kind of blasted past the fields I wanted to use. This wind is *really* fast."

Wick examined their surroundings. The forest went on for a while before it gave way to anything they could land on. It would take several days to get back to their cottage.

"How do we get home?" Wick asked.

"What do you think?" Briar replied. "We walk."

Wick looped an arm around her waist, pulling her close. "You are lucky I enjoy traveling with you."

Briar laughed. She was grinning, but her eyes were soft in a way that stole his breath, even after all this time. She had a lifetime of guarding her heart and had given it to him all the same.

"What is it?" he asked.

She shook her head. "Nothing. Just thinking about how much of my life was traveling, before you. Never stopping. Never settling. And now, I can't wait to get home."

She leaned into him with a happy sigh. Wick nuzzled

her hair, his eyes fixed on her. The sky view was wondrous, but that was nothing compared to his wife's small, contented smile as she thought of their home together.

SPECIAL THANKS

Thank you so much for reading Held!

If you want to support me, please leave a review on Goodreads, Amazon and any social media of your choice.

ACKNOWLEDGMENTS

Firstly, let's hear it for the amazing Kickstarter backers who brought this book to life:

Effy, Megan I, Heather D, Elisha Padilla, Amanda McColly, Makinley Karnivorous, Molly Fessel, Wren Jones, Alaina, Nora, Ashley Bradley, Anonymous, Mistress Sharon, Elizabeth Murphy, Juliana Chiari, Kat Simmons, Christina Getzen, thebiblioaddict, Hailey, Lexi, Iesha Parker-Gask, Raven Friday, Anonymous, Mari T, Daytona M, Kirsty E, Simone Sexton, Megan Long, Nery M Silva, Desiree Montoya-Reeb, Kayla, Zoldos, Amanda Hobbs, Chelsea L, Shelli, Arthur Wilson, Minnie!, Amanda Gauthier, Mandi Corman-Draper, Kaprice Rowe, Shavon Bledsoe, Axel KNG, Katie Yoes, Lexie K, Donna, Stephen B, Dragonskull817.

Now let's hear it for the publishing team! Edward Giordano, formatter extraordinaire, my fabulous editor Naomi Darling, my cover artist Rana Dela (ranadela_x on Instagram), And last but not least, my fantastic beta reader, Matthew (Dragon68).

About the Author

Isabelle Taylor writes sweet, steamy fantasy romance. She works in a bookstore in New Zealand and has a Creative Writing Masters from the International Institute of Modern Letters.

She can be found on Instagram and TikTok @isabelletaylorauthor.

instagram.com/isabelletaylorauthor
tiktok.com/@isabelletaylorauthor